An Inconvenient Marriage

Maria Greene

JOVE BOOKS, NEW YORK

If you purchased this book without a cover, you should be aware that this book is stolen property. It was reported as "unsold and destroyed" to the publisher, and neither the author nor the publisher has received any payment for this "stripped book."

AN INCONVENIENT MARRIAGE

A Jove Book / published by arrangement with
the author

PRINTING HISTORY
Jove edition / March 1994

All rights reserved.
Copyright © 1994 by Maria Greene.
This book may not be reproduced in whole
or in part, by mimeograph or any other means,
without permission. For information address:
The Berkley Publishing Group, 200 Madison Avenue,
New York, New York 10016.

ISBN: 0-515-11336-0

A JOVE BOOK®
Jove Books are published by The Berkley Publishing Group,
200 Madison Avenue, New York, New York 10016.
JOVE and the "J" design are trademarks belonging to
Jove Publications, Inc.

PRINTED IN THE UNITED STATES OF AMERICA

10 9 8 7 6 5 4 3 2 1

Surprising Emotions . . .

"You'll have to be presented at the Queen's Drawing Room before you can attend any functions," the earl pointed out.

Allegra cringed at the thought. "I'm not sure I'm ready to meet the Queen, but a ball is another matter altogether."

"You shall contrive splendidly, my dear. The Queen might be high in the instep, but she's a kind lady . . . Mind you, the ball will be a dead bore. Expect no more than watered sherry and stale cakes for midnight refreshments. Newberry is notoriously tight-fisted."

"We could possibly bring a picnic hamper."

The earl smiled sardonically. "And spread out a tablecloth in the middle of the dance floor . . ." He patted her hand in a brotherly fashion. "You have a lively imagination, Allegra."

They stared at each other for a long moment, and Allegra almost choked on the emotion rising in her chest. She wished she could see love and admiration, not just brotherly approval, in his silver-blue eyes.

The realization jolted her senses. She had to admit to herself that she'd fallen head over heels into love with her husband . . .

Titles by Maria Greene from
The Berkley Publishing Group

DARING GAMBLE
GENTLEMAN BUTLER
LADY IN DISGRACE
LOVER'S KNOT

Dedicated to the members of CNY Romance Writers.
Thank you for your support.

Special thanks to Margaret Benson.

chapter 1

The Earl of Wyndham's head throbbed. His eyes had puffed up so that he could barely see, and his nose had expanded into the semblance of a giant German sausage. At least it felt awkwardly foreign.

He tucked the traveling rug more snugly around his aching, shivering body and applied his handkerchief repeatedly to that congested object in the middle of his face. The drip never stopped, and soon his whole head had swelled to the size of St. Paul's Cathedral stuffed with cotton wool.

Dash it all, but the grippe had caught him unaware. Instead of bumping along a road in his traveling chaise, he should be in a warm bed imbibing hot toddy until sleep took him into sweet oblivion. Yes, oblivion he needed most of all. It would take care of the grippe, as well as the pain in his heart.

Like a dog with his tail tucked between his legs, he'd slunk out of Bath, away from the cruel Miss Justine Bryerly and her tongue that was sharper than a broadsword. The lovely Miss Bryerly, the Incomparable, the most stubborn Miss Bryerly. *Atcchoooo.*

As rain sluiced dismally against the windows, his coach turned onto the London Road. Wyndham coughed and cleared his painful throat. A miserable beggar in the street probably felt a great deal better than he did at this moment.

At any rate, Bath lay behind him, and his future had just started. Some future . . . He sighed and dabbed at his nose. To keep himself outside the pit of despair, he might as well not dwell on the frustrations of the past. His heart would mend in due course, perhaps, but the hollow grief in his chest was another matter. Like acid, the ache fretted his insides, and the thought of returning to the hollow tomb of a mansion that was his home in Berkley Square did not attract. Not with this added pain of the heart; it was a pain he'd never experienced before.

He'd not suspected Justine would jilt him, not when he'd honestly bared the depth of his feelings. But Justine evidently loved another—the Marquess of Lewington—who was a damned cold fish, and cunning to boot.

Wyndham shrugged mentally, trying to shake off his gloomy thoughts. He despised self-pity in others and loathed himself for succumbing to this pathetic weakness. He trumpeted into his handkerchief, and loathed himself even more.

He'd been unable to convince Justine that Lewington would hurt her—squander her money, then discard her at the crumbling Lewington country seat to rear the Lewington offspring. She would be bored to flinders. When she discovered the marquess's true side, it would be too late. It pained Wyndham to watch her make the mistake of her life; it hurt damnably. . . .

The tedious thoughts tumbled and cavorted, grating on his mind; they would not leave him alone. Haunting visions of the headstrong, lovely Justine disturbed his peace. . . .

With a shuddering sigh and another explosive sneeze, he closed his eyes in the darkness. If only he could sleep, and not awaken until they reached the capital. By then he might be able to see a slight glimmer of hope for the future.

Damn it all to hell. His skin had turned clammy with fever, and dizziness seized him. Mayhap the grippe would be the end of him. By Jove, that would be one way out of his misery, he thought with a cynical twist of his parched lips. His insides seemed to be on fire, and a giant was pounding his brain into mash.

Good! the end was near. With that thought, he finally collapsed.

The cold rain oozed through Allegra Temple's thin kid slippers and slithered under the tarpaulin below which she was hiding. Her pelisse, once a respectable article of twilled sarcenet, now clung sodden to her body, and before long, the wetness would reach her skin. Her other garments, thin muslin gown, petticoat, and shift, were poor armor against the weather. She shivered as an icy droplet stabbed her cheek. Surreptitiously, she wiped away a hot tear—the only warm item within reaching distance.

Coaches rumbled into the yard of the posting inn at Chippenham, every one heading in the wrong direction. A perishing night to be abroad, she thought. Unless she could conjure up some hidden power to change the weather, she would have to endure until the rain let up and the clouds dispersed. As far as she could tell, she had no magical powers, only the common variety of luck. No matter how entreatingly she looked at the sky and touched the four-leaf clover in its locket pinned to her bodice, the gods did not show any mercy, and Lady Fortune had turned away for the time being.

Allegra had fled before it was too late, before Stepfather could force her to marry their lecherous neighbor, Ezra Skelton. If only she were of age, she could go against Stepfather's wishes. But barely eighteen, she was a chattel of Mr. Woodruff Pinkney to dispose of as he wished. While her mother reclined most of her days on a chaise longue, reading and eating bonbons, Woodruff saw about gaining ever more influence in the Chippenham area. He'd schemed and snaked himself into every pocket that held some degree of affluence, and he'd decided that Allegra would marry Ezra Skelton, whose land marched cheek by jowl with Temple meadows. Before long, the Skelton acres would be part of Woodruff's empire—*if* she married Ezra. That, she never would.

Why, she would rather become a nun, even though the thought held little allure.

Really, running away had been her only choice, a choice that had brought her to this point of water-logged misery.

Her teeth chattered, and her hands had turned numb with cold. "No help in sight, but don't lose hope," she whispered to herself. "Something is bound to turn up." Luck had always been on her side. Hadn't she found the four-leaf clover last summer?

Most likely, she would have to suffer until morning before a London-bound carriage arrived, but she would survive. She *would*. Everyone said—or complained—that she had Papa's stubborn streak.

Worry tightened in her stomach, and she curled her arms around her knees to stop them from knocking together. If she didn't find someone to give her a coach seat, she might have to face the possible risk of her stepfather finding her. After all, she had put no more than two miles between herself and the man she detested most in this world. Soon daylight would arrive, and she would be unable to hide as easily.

She'd had enough courage to stand up to Woodruff, to tell him she had no intention of marrying Skelton. Now she had to pay for her rebellion in misery. She wished she'd had the time to gather some clothes and some money before she fled, but it had been only a matter of minutes before Skelton arrived to perform the charade of offering for her hand.

In her mind, she saw Ezra's sweaty hands close around her arm, and his gaze rove upon her body. She shuddered at the memory. She had made the excuse to her stepfather that she wanted to freshen up, then slipped on pelisse and bonnet, climbed through her bedroom window, and slid down the trunk of a big oak. Having learned the trick from her brother Giles, she could scale any tree with ease.

With the urgent need to get away, she had run into the woods without any thoughts to bodily comforts.

Her tears mingled with the rain on her face. She dashed them off with an angry twist of her hand. *Don't be such a watering pot.* Tears would not bring her closer to London and Aunt Irene's house in Half Moon Street. What would bring her closer was a carriage heading for the Metropolis. She'd had dratted bad luck all night. Bound to change any time, though. If only she'd brought her pin money, she could have bought a seat on the stagecoach.

Some unseen animal scurried among the sticks in the woodpile behind her. She shuddered with revulsion and shot a desperate glance toward the dreary inn yard. No coaches had stopped after midnight. Only a patch of yellow light from inside the main building illuminated the area. The smell of damp earth and wet wood filled her nose. The wood stump on which she was sitting made her backside numb. She shifted her feet in hope of finding a dryer spot, but only managed to put them into a deeper puddle of water.

Pulling the pelisse more tightly around her shivering body, she tried to prop her back against the wall of the shed beside which the woodpile leaned, but the wall was slippery with moisture.

The rain finally slowed to a drizzle. The world held its

breath as if every soul in the vicinity was asleep. Allegra's head tilted forward until her chin touched her chest. She dozed in fits and starts.

With a twitch she awakened as something jumped onto her lap. She gasped in fear, then relaxed as she heard a distinct purr. A sodden kitten, fur ragged, tail like a stringy rope. Its tiny heart raced as Allegra put her hand around the meager chest. It butted her hand with a cold wet nose, and Allegra did not have the heart to push it down. She held it close to her chest to induce some warmth to the shivering body. The kitten purred harder and tried to burrow deeper within the sodden folds of her pelisse. Poor beggar, lonely and starved. Allegra could count all the ribs, and the backbone arched like a series of hard knobs.

She patted the kitten, trying to gauge how long she'd slept. On the east horizon the sky had turned a dull gray. Dawn would soon arrive. Still holding the kitten, she stood, stretching her legs. Her stomach growled, and she contemplated sneaking into the inn's kitchen and stealing some food. Without food she would grow light-headed. Since she'd been unable to find a place in a coach destined for London, she ought to start walking east. It would not do to linger too close to home and Woodruff Pinkney.

She peeked around the edge of the stiff tarpaulin. Nothing moved except a big white cock scratching in the mud, its red wattle wobbling. Soon enough he would tilt his head back and herald the new day. Worried that someone would see her and recognize her, she stepped away from her hiding place.

Just as she slunk toward the kitchen entrance still clutching the kitten, she heard the rumble of a vehicle on the road. She dashed back under the tarpaulin just as a coach-and-four entered the muddy yard.

The coachman, dressed in a heavy cloak and a hat pulled low over his ears, hauled in the reins. The horses trampled the ground nervously, and Allegra watched the carriage with great interest. The door displayed a crest, but she did not recognize it. Evidently the equipage was heading toward London.

The leather curtains had been pulled in front of the windows, and Allegra assumed the occupants were asleep.

The coachman got down from the box and stretched his stubby legs. From the stables a half-dressed ostler staggered into the yard, yawning. The coachman greeted him in a loud voice.

"Fresh 'orses, me good fellow, and do not tarry."

"Goin' t' Lunnon?" the ostler asked as he released the horses from the shackles.

Holding her breath, Allegra waited for the coachman's answer.

"Aye, that we are. To London town. Is there a drop o' ale to be 'ad in this establishment?"

The ostler replied, "Certainly. Go up an' knock on the kitchen door. The maid will let ye in."

The coachman betook himself to the main building, and the ostler led the tired horses to the stables.

Without letting herself hesitate once, Allegra made a move toward the coach. She heard no sounds from inside the vehicle. She tried to peer in the crack between the curtain and the window frame, but could only see blackness.

Her heart hammering with suspense, she gently eased the door open. She muttered a word of gratitude as the hinges moved without shrieking.

She glanced inside quickly. A long bundle on one of the seats captured her attention. Someone was sleeping under a stack of traveling rugs and a many-caped driving coat. Not a sound issued from the person. The opposite seat was empty.

Without further ado, she stepped inside and closed the door softly behind her. Whoever was sleeping so peacefully would get a dreadful shock upon awakening, but that problem would have to be solved later. She would explain her predicament, and Aunt Irene would certainly reimburse the person whose carriage brought her niece to London. Allegra had no doubt that she was doing the right thing. Only daring would help her out of this latest pickle. She realized that she was still clutching the kitten. Too late to let it off now. She didn't dare open the door again lest someone discover her.

As the kitten curled into a ball in her lap, she waited with a pounding heart for the coachman to return. Would he look inside and find her? The ostler put a new team between the shackles, and the carriage rocked with the movements of the horses.

A handful of minutes later she heard male voices discussing the weather outside. She drew a sigh of relief as the weight of the coachman sent the carriage tilting as he stepped onto the box. He hadn't looked inside.

Allegra shot a glance at the figure on the opposite seat. She wondered which end was the head. If only the bundle were a lady, but the absence of a maid told her otherwise. The many-caped coat hinted that the traveler was most certainly a gentleman.

That realization disturbed her no end. What if he was the worst rake in London? A gambler and a libertine? Someone worse than Ezra Skelton? Filled with uncertainty, she chewed on her bottom lip. She had very little experience with gentlemen.

The coach moved out of the inn yard, and the prostrate figure started fighting with the rugs. A long muscular arm emerged, and a guttural moan came from under the covers. Allegra shrunk into the corner of her seat. A strong bronzed hand flexed, then a head of short black waves appeared. He shook his head and coughed but didn't open his eyes.

In the weak light of dawn filtering into the coach, Allegra studied the virile face of the stranger. He appeared to carry some twenty-seven or -eight years on his shoulders. The lean cheeks were flushed either with drink or fever, and curling lashes shaded the dark hollows under his eyes. The long thin nose had a reddish hue, and the pugnacious jaw held a shading of dark stubble. His attractive lips looked white and stiff with pain.

The gentleman with morning whiskers made a strangely intimate picture, and Allegra blushed in her corner. She had never seen a man asleep before, and she wondered if her choice to jump into this particular carriage had been a grand mistake. He opened his eyes, but it was too dark for her to see their color. He stared straight at her and said,

"Justine, what in the world are you doing here? Didn't you just throw me out on my ear?"

Allegra started with guilt. Evidently the stranger could not see her very well in the semidarkness. He sounded as if he was suffering from a tremendous cold, but his voice was cultured, imperious, that of an aristocrat. His clothing, what she could see of it, displayed a subdued elegance.

"Why so silent?" he inquired hoarsely and struggled to sit up. With a groan he collapsed before he'd managed to get onto his elbow. "Are you here to give me another rakedown? As if the one you gave me didn't suffice. You shredded my heart!" That pronouncement ended with a sneeze.

"I . . . I was wool-gathering," Allegra whispered, praying that he wouldn't realize that she wasn't Justine. Justine . . . Allegra wondered if he meant Justine Bryerly, her old friend from the genteel lady's academy in Bath. *I would have known Justine better if Stepfather hadn't decided to interrupt my schooling and haul me back to Temple Manor. . . .*

"Come closer," the stranger demanded. "I can't see you very well."

Allegra leaned forward reluctantly. With some luck he wouldn't notice that she wasn't Justine.

His breathing rattled and he got into a fit of coughing. She thought it might finish him off, but the attack subsided at last. Thank God, he was too weak to pursue his acquaintance with her. A moment later a snore issued from his mouth.

With a sigh of relief Allegra sank back into her corner and caressed the kitten. If the gentleman slept until the coach arrived in London, she might disappear without another confrontation.

She'd dozed for what seemed half an hour when a drawn-out moan awakened her. Her eyes widened as she tried to get her bearings. The well-sprung carriage was hurtling along at a spanking pace. Dawn had taken on a rosy tint, predicting the imminent sunrise. Allegra glanced at the prostrate gentleman and realized the moans were issuing from him. He thrashed about, and if she didn't do something, he would roll to the floor.

Allegra set down the kitten and moved to the opposite seat. Gingerly, she lifted the gentleman's head into her lap. She didn't know what to do if he awakened, but his obvious suffering kindled her compassion. He was in urgent need of tender care, and perhaps she could provide some solace.

Tentatively she caressed the wavy hair that felt springy as moss, yet soft as silk under her fingers. His skin clammy, he was burning up with fever. As she continued to caress him, he quieted down. A long sigh quivered on his lips, and Allegra felt a curious tenderness in her heart. This was the first time she'd been close to a gentleman stranger. She had touched her brother's hair, but it was soft and fine, like a female's, like her own. This gentleman's hair felt resilient and virile, exciting. She blushed at that shocking thought. *Mother would be scandalized if she were here, but in truth she rarely approves of anything I do.* Allegra caressed the dark head in her lap more vigorously.

He made a grunt of contentment, then stiffened under her hand. Allegra flinched as if slapped when he opened his eyes and stared straight at her. She noticed that he had silvery blue eyes, and they blazed now. She hazarded a guess that fever made them glow, but it could just as easily be anger. She might as well try to make him understand.

"Please, sir ... let me explain," she said uncertainly.

"What the devil?" he croaked. "You're not Justine. Who are you, and what are you doing in my carriage?" His body convulsed in a sneeze. He pressed a handkerchief to his nose and glared at her with watery eyes.

"Traveling," she said with a show of flippancy that was as sheer as gossamer. "From Chippenham to London."

He tried to remove his head from her lap, but clearly it was too much of an effort. He slumped back, glaring at her. Embarrassed, she looked everywhere except at him.

"You were having a nightmare, and I thought I could help," she explained. She had no idea what to do with her hands now. It wouldn't do to continue caressing his hair.

"It seems that I'm still in the middle of that nightmare," he spat. Another sneeze blunted his angry remark.

"Well, you are not. If it wasn't for me, you would have rolled onto the floor and perhaps hurt yourself."

His lips quirked cynically. "Thank you, Miss .... or is it Mrs.? I'm deeply and eternally grateful."

"It's Miss Temple, Allegra Temple."

"I ought to make a gallant bow, but under the present circumstances I must decline." His chiding voice set her teeth on edge.

"No need to be sarcastic."

"Why am I driving through the night with a stranger in my traveling chaise? I do not recall inviting you."

"You are too ill to remember," she lied, then regretted the falsehood. "No ... as a matter of fact, I sneaked in when you were asleep. I'm most desperate to get to London. Any conveyance with that destination—"

"And you chose mine." A sharp edge crept into his voice. "I should be honored."

"No need to get in high dudgeon over this. Once we reach the Capital, I will take myself off your hands." Allegra thought she sounded more sure of herself than she felt inside.

"Highly considerate of you, Miss Temple." His voice blurred, and two red spots glowed on his cheeks.

"I would pay for my seat, but unfortunately I don't have a groat to my name."

He laughed hollowly. "Surely it's worth more than a groat."

Anger was starting to churn in her chest. "A true gentleman would be honored to aid a damsel in distress."

"A *knight* might have been that foolish, but this is 1816, not the Middle Ages. In fact, you have saddled me with a deuced problem. I ought to convey you back to Chippenham, or at least see to it that you get on the westbound stage. If someone sees you here with me, your reputation will be ruined."

"Who is going to see us at this early hour?" Allegra scoffed.

"I asked Tripp to halt for breakfast at Hungerford. You must stay concealed, or better yet, let's part company there. I shall endeavor to hire an equipage for you, and a maid to lend you respectability."

She plucked at the damp fabric of her pelisse. "*No!* No, sir, I can't be beholden to you. *Please* ... You can't leave me stranded in a strange village. I'll be quiet as a mouse all the way to London. You won't notice my presence further." She glanced at the sleeping kitten from the corner of her eye. To her relief she noticed that it sported a black silky coat that blended well with the dark upholstery.

The stranger swore under his breath, and she sensed that he wouldn't be adverse to flinging her out the door this very minute.

"I'm only trying to protect you from wagging tongues, Miss Temple, but I suppose it's too late for that now." He spoke with difficulty as if too tired to move his lips. "You have launched yourself upon the world without chaperon and sufficient funds. A reckless action by anyone's standards. Very well, it's not my place to give you a beargarden jaw, but I ask you to reconsider my offer."

Allegra sniffed. "You have no idea what made me 'launch myself upon the world,' so I beg of you to withhold your scathing remarks." She was rapidly losing her patience with the gentleman. "You nag more than my grandmother used to, rest her soul."

He mumbled something under his breath, but she could not discern the words. His eyes fluttered shut, and she noticed that the dark hollows below the lashes had deepened.

She realized that he was about to fall asleep. The fever had weakened him, and as his body battled the sickness, he had no strength left to throw her off the coach. Thank Heaven for that, she thought. His head still rested in her lap, but she avoided touching him since that seemed to set off his temper.

She couldn't blame him for his anger. If the grippe had ravaged her like it had him, she might be inclined to show her ill temper. Thankful of her good fortune, she decided to forgive the stranger for his irritability. Soon enough their paths would part.

When the carriage halted at the next posting inn, the sun had crept above the horizon, splashing the landscape with pink gold. Allegra looked outside. Birds chirped in the trees, and kittens cavorted on the steps leading to the inn.

Hers was still asleep. What induced her to keep the kitten? Hadn't she problems enough?

A maid was beating a rug in the yard. She glanced at the carriage curiously, and Allegra drew back. The gentleman, whose head had lolled sideways on her thigh, had warned her that to be seen equaled a ruinous reputation. He was right, of course.

Tripp opened the door and peered inside. As his gaze lit upon her, his mouth fell open in shock, and he flinched back.

"Good morning," she greeted in a faltering voice. "Your master is very sick."

"Miss," he muttered and fluttered his hands. Evidently he was in a quandary about what to do next. "The master will want a glass o' ale afore we go on. 'Is Lor'ship exspecially told me to wake 'im at Hungerford if 'e were asleep."

Allegra lifted the stranger's limp head off her thigh and moved across to the opposite seat. She scooped up the kitten and said nothing, only watched as the coachman, whose bulbous nose was dripping just like his master's, shook the hard shoulder protruding from the rugs.

"Yer Lor'ship, we're in Hungerford. Time fer breakfast."

His Lordship muttered something and tossed his head back and forth. A cough racked his body, and compassion filled Allegra's heart.

"Mark me words, 'e'll 'ave inflammation o' the lungs afore the week is over," Tripp said.

"Who is this gentleman?" Allegra asked.

"Who? Why, miss, don't ye know ye be travelin' wi' 'Is Lor'ship, the Earl o' Wynd'am? I'm a mite confused as to the exact spot we met up with yer young person, miss." He glanced at Allegra expectantly, but she refused to enlighten him.

Ian Royden, the Earl of Wyndham, she thought. She knew of him. The proud Wyndhams hailed from a village east of Bath, Bradford-on-Avon, and she remembered that her father had spoken highly of the family. How he'd made the acquaintance of the earl, or the earl's father, she didn't know.

Wyndham roused himself out of his stupor sufficiently to glare at her.

"I see that you're still here," he said threateningly, and Allegra glanced guiltily to the floor. She trembled with apprehension. He would surely throw her off the coach now, kitten and all.

The earl took one look at the yawning kitten, swore under his breath, and swung his legs out the door. Perspiration glistened on his forehead, and Allegra sensed his tremendous effort to remain upright. He possessed a magnificent body, tall and muscular, and *daunting*.

He stepped down on wobbly legs, and Tripp steadied one arm. The earl's clothing, coat of blue superfine and pale yellow pantaloons, looked sadly rumpled, but Allegra noted the flawless tailoring and the gleaming leather of his Hessian boots. The earl raked a hand through his hair as if to make himself more presentable, but it only made him look worse.

"May'ap I should get ye the ale and bring it out," Tripp suggested. "Ye're weak as a kitten."

"No! *Do not* mention kittens.... I need to stretch my legs. My whole body aches, but I'll be damned if I'll stay cooped up in the chaise like an old woman."

Allegra bristled at that, suspecting he'd insulted her with his careless words. She glanced toward the inn where nothing moved.

After settling her furry traveling companion on the seat, she stepped down. No one would notice her, she told herself. Her reputation was safe in this village. She shook out her wrinkled pelisse and untied the faded ribbons of her straw bonnet. Perhaps she could find a place to freshen up. Her hair needed untangling, and her face could use a good wash.

Leaning on Tripp's shoulders, the earl staggered forward. Tripp stood a whole head shorter than his master, and he could barely support the younger man. They stumbled, and both would have fallen if Allegra hadn't run forward to support the earl on the other side.

"This is folly, Lord Wyndham. You must return to your carriage before you fall into a faint."

"I need to relieve—" the earl blurted out, but he didn't have the strength to finish the sentence. A bit embarrassed, he glared at Allegra. "I told you to stay . . . inside."

Allegra refused to move. Leaning heavily on her shoulder and Tripp's, the earl tottered toward the steps leading to the taproom. The door opened, and a group of people emerged, staring down at them.

Allegra raised her head and glanced at the door. She expected to see the proprietor of the inn, or a maid, but only the hard scrutiny of ladies dressed in silk pelisses and plumed bonnets met her gaze.

She gasped and almost lost hold of her burden. A lady she knew from Chippenham, Mrs. Lucrezia Fishwood, gave her a high-bred stare through a quizzing glass.

"Well! It is Miss Temple, isn't it?" she asked in freezing tones. "And who is your inebriated gentleman companion?"

Before Allegra could reply, another lady said, "It's Ian Royden, the Earl of Wyndham."

"Thank you, Mrs. Drummond-Burrell," Mrs. Fishwood said triumphantly. She turned her gaze on Allegra. "I must say I'm frightfully shocked to find you in the arms of a stranger at dawn. Your mother will have a violent fit of the vapors when she hears about this."

chapter 2

Wyndham opened his aching eyes and focused on the ceiling, which seemed to undulate like the waves in the sea. He couldn't recall a time when he'd felt more poorly. His throat ... his head ... his stomach—every part had decided to work against him.

Was he back home then, in the silent tomb that still echoed with the cold voice of his departed father?

Wyndham grimaced. He realized he was lying on a lumpy mattress, a moldy and itchy blanket pulled up to his chin. A nervous movement beside him stated that he wasn't alone in the room. He turned his head, a painful ordeal that didn't improve his temper one whit.

With aching gritty eyes, he stared at the young woman perching on a three-legged stool beside him. Wavy brown hair, which had loosened from an untidy chignon, framed her worried oval face. He halted for a moment, wondering why she bore such an apprehensive expression, then his gaze traveled on. He was too tired to think. Her complexion had the fine texture of silk, a pale pink rose. Her blue muslin dress looked bedraggled, but that did not detract from her gentle beauty. A long neck, a tall slender frame, ears like pink shells. Such an innocent picture she made. No hint of cunningness marred her features, yet the vixen had contrived to sneak into his coach and set him up for scandal. Her brow furrowed in worry, and as she glanced at him, he noticed fear darkening the sky-blue eyes.

"Oh, you're awake then," she said and started to pleat the material of her gown frantically. "Feeling any better?"

"Are you still here?" His own voice grated on his ears, and his headache grew worse. "I thought we would part. I distinctly remember that I asked Tripp to arrange—or maybe I only thought—" Cursing his weakness, he tried to raise himself on one elbow, but a warm weight on his torso held him back. He glanced down at himself, finding a black furry shape curled on his chest.

"What the deuce!" he croaked, and the feline turned sleepy content eyes on him.

"Beau likes you. As soon as he'd lapped his milk, he jumped up and settled on your chest. Has been there for hours."

"And you let him stay?"

"Tripp thought the warmth might help to fend off inflammation of the lungs. I agree. My grandmother used to put a cat skin on my back every time I had the cough. There's nothing like it for warmth. The tiger-striped is the best kind, Grandmama used to say, rest her soul."

Wyndham shivered in disgust. "Nonsense!"

"Besides," she added sagely, "a living cat must work ever so much better—even if Beau's only a kitten. You'll be more like yourself in no time at all."

The earl realized he had the harrowing choice of shoving the tiny fur ball to the floor or jeopardizing his life. The kitten stayed.

"Where are we?" he asked when he was able to push aside his anger enough to speak.

"In Hungerford."

He lay his head back down, contemplating the fact. "I thought we'd—or I'd—be in London by now."

"You were too sick to go on."

Filled with suspicion, he glared at her. "Where's Tripp, and why haven't you left the inn?"

"There ... were no other coaches to London, and I couldn't very well leave you in the midst of your illness. That would have been excessively selfish of me."

He sighed, wondering if she was having a private joke at his expense, but he couldn't detect any hint of unholy glee in her sky-blue eyes. "There must be coaches going back and forth every day."

He fumbled for his coat on the chair beside the bed and found it gone. "You'll find a purse in my pocket. Help yourself to enough funds to pay for a stagecoach ticket back to Chippenham. In this sorry state, I can't help you personally; otherwise I would. Tripp can escort you back to your home."

He closed his eyes and fought the weakness threatening to overcome him. Somehow the immediate problems had grown too big to handle from his sickbed. By God, he had to get up! The thought ended in a violent fit of coughing. The kitten dug its claws into him, and he was ready to wring Beau's—*Beau's! Faugh!*—miserable neck right then and there. Fortunately for the kitten, the resourceful Miss Temple lifted him off the heaving ship of a chest.

"The maid will bring up a posset. It will relieve your fever and your coughing."

He recalled getting off the coach and seeing some shadowy figures talking on the front steps. A terrible foreboding came over him. "Miss Temple, just whom did we meet this morning?"

"Yesterday morning, you mean?" Her voice trembled, and he noticed the misery in her eyes. Her hands traveled nervously back and forth over the kitten's back.

"Yesterday? You've been with me all this time?"

"I worried about you. I felt it was my fault. . . . I

couldn't just leave you . . . to carry the burden alone." Her voice petered out. "Anyway, Beau needed his milk."

"What by the devil are you talking about?" he asked testily, as the knowledge of impending doom shredded his patience.

A fat tear rolled down her cheek, and her incredibly vulnerable lips trembled. He softened. "Don't cry. I'm sorry I used language not fit for a lady's ear. My patience is frayed at best. What is the matter?"

"I . . . *we* were spotted." She heaved a deep sigh. "I've never been more mortified. Mrs. Lucrezia Fishwood *and* Mrs. Drummond-Burrell saw us together. You had, ahem, an arm draped around my shoulder."

Despite his foreboding, her words hit him harder than a real blow to his solar plexus would. As his mind sorted through the shrinking vista of possibilities, he had a sinking feeling in his stomach. He dreaded her next words and clenched his hands into fists.

"Mrs. Fishwood knows my mother. When my parents find out the truth, they'll follow me to the ends of the earth and *surely* make me go back home and marry Ezra Skelton. I'd rather be dead. In fact, I think I shall kill myself, throw myself into the nearest river."

"Don't be a goose," he snapped. "Are you sure the ladies recognized us?"

She nodded miserably. "Mrs. Drummond-Burrell said your name."

He groaned. "She's the highest stickler for propriety. You're ruined, Miss Temple, ruined beyond redemption." He wanted to shout at her, but his voice was no more than a croak. Besides, she looked so damned innocent with her guileless blue eyes and tears streaming down her cheeks. He felt an inexplicable urge to wipe them off. He ought to feel the urge to wring, not only the kitten's neck, but hers as well.

"I know it was totty-headed to show myself in broad daylight unchaperoned, but you would have hurt yourself, and Tripp, if you'd fallen to the ground. I couldn't just stand by and watch. I . . ." Her worried voice faltered.

A band of dread tightened around his chest. "Don't get into a lather, Miss Temple. We shall think of something to get us out of this pickle."

He turned his head on the pillow and stared toward the grimy window. The daylight hurt his eyes, and thoughts tumbled in his mind, circling the question to which he already had the dreadful answer. He kept silent, seeking desperately for some other solution, thinking of plausible explanations. But he knew truly only one honorable way to solve this dashed problem.

As a gentleman, he would have to marry the chit. Caught in a mousetrap, by God. As the dread in his heart tightened further, he threw a contemptuous glance at her. Might as well bring it up before he fainted with fatigue. He wished he didn't feel so sadly out of curl.

He had to offer for her. Perhaps she would rather die than marry him. The flare of hope crumpled as soon as it'd been born. What female in her right mind—or wrong for that matter—would turn down the chance of a title and a fortune? Matchmaking mamas had hounded him in vain, and now a country chit had snared him as easily as if he were a brainless rabbit.

"Do dry your tears, Miss Temple. I will do the honorable thing, of course. That is, give you the protection of my name." He sighed. "Not . . . that I much enjoy the thought at this juncture, but I see no other way."

He ruminated for a moment, wondering if he'd been too hasty. But if he couldn't have Justine Bryerly, he might as well marry anyone. This innocent was as good as any, he thought dispiritedly. Perhaps the union would save them both, her from an unwanted marriage, and him from a long bout of hoping for what he would not have. Might as well nip his desperate longing for Justine in the bud before it overwhelmed him.

"I'm ashamed to admit that I've forgotten your name, miss."

"Allegra Temple."

"Are you the daughter of Sir Edwin Temple?"

She nodded. "Yes."

"My father and yours were friends at one time. I'd like to think I could do Sir Edwin a favor. He would have expected me to protect you, to do the right thing. He would expect—"

"You don't love me," she said in a small voice.

"You're right on that score. We might as well be honest with each other rather than pretend that our union will be anything more than a marriage of convenience."

"Convenient at first perhaps, but highly inconvenient in the passing of time." She straightened her drooping head and gave him a willful stare. "I cannot marry you."

"Why not?" he asked, his anger stirring. "A lady could not make a better match."

"Be that as it may, I do not find myself transported into bliss by your offer." She sniffed into her handkerchief, and Wyndham wanted to shake some sense into her.

"Confound it all," he muttered. "You'll have to marry me, and that's the end of it." Watching her stubborn chin through a haze of anger, he added, "Any fool could point out the merits of this union."

"I'm not a fool." She blew her nose, and Wyndham found himself longing to kick a wall or something equally hard.

He turned over on the cot, facing the window. "You'll come to your senses in due time. You should rejoice. Many a young lady would not reject the offer of wealth and a title."

"I don't give a fig for the lofty appendix to your name, milord."

"That was a dashed paltry thing to say, Miss Temple."

Drained, and his anger banked to a slow—if hot—fire, he couldn't make himself talk anymore. He drifted off to sleep thinking that Miss Temple had none of Justine's flair. Justine was lost forever. He'd just burned all his bridges. Come to think of it, his offer to marry the twit had been a rather harrowing ordeal that he might have found a way to avoid, had not his wits been so befuddled with fever.

Allegra stared at the broad back and stifled an urge to stick out her tongue. The arrogant earl thought she would fall to her knees in gratitude! She couldn't care less about position and wealth. Romantic at heart, she'd hoped to marry a gentleman who had some tender feelings toward her, someone who would love and cherish her forever.

The earl had offered his name as if it were a necessary attribute to their business transaction—as if they had one. She hadn't promised anything.

As she listened to his soft snore, she had to get up and pace lest she slam the broth bowl into his skull. She'd worried about his illness for a day and night, with barely any sleep to restore her spirits. When he'd awakened, all he'd seen was a humble dog that should be thrown the bone of his title and his wealth. Here, country mutt, have my title and be proud of it! If he had known how difficult it had been only to ask for a seat to London!

Allegra thought she would explode with frustration, but when the earl awakened at nightfall, she sat in stony silence, staring at him. He stared back.

"Well, have you had enough time to think about my offer?" he said as Tripp gingerly helped him pull on his coat.

"I didn't need time to think about it. The answer is still no, and always will be. Just put me down in Half Moon

Street when we arrive in London, and you will never have to see me again."

He only shook his head and laughed mirthlessly. With a sinking feeling, she knew his was the right way, that he might win in the end. But not without a fight.

Allegra knocked on the front door of Aunt Irene's town house in Half Moon Street. It was a tall white building squeezed between a house festooned with Baroque plaster garlands and a residence with bulging bow windows. Hunger and exhaustion dragged her down, and her clothing had seen better days. Not to mention her hair. But since misery occupied every corner of her mind, she barely registered the sad state of her appearance.

"Truly, I didn't plan to make trouble for anyone," she whispered to the kitten as a footman opened the door. Standing behind the lackey, a thin butler with a long mournful face stared down his nose at her.

"Wiggins, isn't it? I would like to see Mrs. Sinclair. I'm her niece, Miss Temple." She took a step up, and the butler reluctantly let her into the minute hallway.

"Please wait here, Miss Temple. I don't know if Mrs. Sinclair is admitting visitors. It is rather early to pay social calls, don't you think?" He glanced at her rumpled garments, and a disapproving frown appeared between his white eyebrows. Yet, he returned five minutes later and ushered her up the stairs to the morning room. She deposited Beau into Wiggins's reluctant gloved hands. "Feed him, please, and don't let him outside."

Irene Sinclair had the wiry build of a lady who favored vigorous horseback exercise every day. She rose from her breakfast tray and descended upon Allegra with her arms held out. "Oh, dearest girl, you gave me quite a turn by appearing on my doorstep unannounced."

She embraced Allegra, who struggled against a torrent

of tears. The last two days had been almost too much strain for her. Now she felt safe—at last. She sobbed against Aunt Irene's sturdy shoulder. "I've run away from home."

Irene gasped and turned her blue eyes to her niece's face. Her warm smile clouded with distress. "Dear child, what did you say?"

Aunt Irene had aged. The dark short curls were heavily laced with gray, and wrinkles had appeared around the clear, wise eyes. Aunt Irene reminded Allegra of Father; the same kind blue eyes looked at her, the same button nose seemed more at home on Irene's face than it had on her father's. As if ready to go out for her morning ride, her aunt wore a smart brown riding habit trimmed with gold braiding and epaulets.

"Yes, I've run away, Aunt Irene, and I've made a complete muddle of things."

"Come and sit down before you fall into a swoon. You look worn to a shade. You shall have a cup of tea to strengthen your spirit, and then you shall tell me the whole."

Aunt Irene turned to the butler standing by the door with the wiggling kitten in his arms. "Bring in a fresh pot of tea, Wiggins, then take yourself off for the morning. We don't want to be disturbed."

Ten minutes later Allegra was sipping hot tea and nibbling on a slice of buttered toast. Her spirits somewhat restored, she launched into her story.

"Oh, Auntie, I've never been in such a quandary. You don't know Pinkney as I do, but believe me, he is the most horrid, the most *grasping* person alive. As you must recall, he was father's banker, a mushroom of the worst kind, who insinuated himself into Mother's life when Papa died."

"Dearest child, Honoria is not a person who can live

alone. She needs the strong shoulder of a husband to lean on."

Allegra said heatedly, "Yes, but she has dubious taste. I could have sworn Mr. Pinkney had his eye on Mother for a long time, even before Father died, and the attraction seemed mutual." She set down her cup and twisted her fingers together to stop them from trembling. "When they married, I felt as if Mother abandoned me. She cares for no one but Pinkney and his welfare. He demands utter devotion."

"Did you tell her about your feelings?"

"I've been unable to reveal my problems in depth," Allegra said and averted her eyes. It pained her to disclose her despair and make her mother into a villain, but Irene might understand. She had understood, just as Allegra had learned, that the marriage between Sir Edwin and Honoria had been an unhappy union. "She complained about my 'rebellious spirit'—as she called it."

"What did she say exactly?" Irene poured more tea for her niece and stirred a generous amount of sugar into the cup.

"She accused me of being jealous of Pinkney, who has taken the place of my beloved father. She said I would get used to the situation in due course."

"Maybe you would have. A stepfather is difficult to accept, especially for someone at your *advanced* age." Aunt Irene's eyes twinkled briefly, and Allegra wished she could see the humor of the situation.

"There's some truth to that, but it isn't the whole truth. In fact, Mother is besotted with her cunning new husband—Papa's direct opposite, dark and saturnine where Papa was pale and gentle-faced. Somehow she lost her very identity to Pinkney, becoming a stranger to Giles and me. Stepfather has a *way* with Mama."

"Mr. Pinkney is a pompous fool," Irene said with conviction. "I thought so at the wedding, and I'm sure he lost no time stepping into your father's shoes."

"On the very first day he resided at Temple Manor, he warned me that he would find a way to scour the hoydenish ways from my character. He said that Father had been much too lenient with Giles and me. He threatened that he would bring me to heel."

"I see. Marriage to an older gentleman would be the means," Irene muttered with a frown.

"Yes, a suitable husband would be found posthaste, and that would be the end of my wild ways."

Allegra sipped her tea agitatedly, then set down her cup so hard that liquid slopped over the side. "Auntie, Pinkney *loomed* over me and said he would not accept a stepdaughter who was a walking embarrassment to him."

"The fool! He humiliated you."

"He accused me of deliberately dressing as a servant, said I had no style. Auntie, it was a declaration of war. 'I can't very well buy a new wardrobe with the pittance you give me,' I said to him."

"Nor could you. A veritable skinflint, Mr. Pinkney. A common trait in bankers."

Allegra still remembered every nuance of his expression. He had opened and closed his mouth in shock. For her mother's sake, she had tried to keep the peace, sometimes succeeding, sometimes failing. Her temper had its shortcomings, but mostly she tried to be good-natured and optimistic. If only Mother had taken some interest, chosen to support her at times, life would have been easier. But she had never listened, only agreed with Pinkney in all things.

Stepfather might have schemed his way into the banking business, then into Mother's affections, but his humble birth was the greatest grievance of his life. He always strived for ways to better himself. Allegra doubted that

Stepfather was capable of loving anyone but himself and the money that had come into his greedy hands upon his marriage to Mother.

She told Irene about the loathsome Ezra Skelton, about the rain and the night she spent under the tarpaulin. When she came to the part of Wyndham's coach and the appearance of Mesdames Fishwood and Drummond-Burrell, her voice faltered.

"Oh, Aunt, I've made the worst mull of things. The earl would have sent me back home if he weren't so ill," she explained. "Then he said my reputation was in shreds and that I had to marry him. He's a cold fish, offered me his name as if it meant nothing to him. I was mortified."

Irene clasped her hands to her bosom. "Oh, dear, this is the most dreadful story I've ever heard. I fear I will have a fit of palpitations."

Allegra's spirits plummeted. "Mrs. Fishwood evidently thought I was eloping with Lord Wyndham. Furthermore, she accused Lord Wyndham of being in his cups, which couldn't have been further from the truth. He floundered in the throes of a horrid grippe."

Aunt Irene gulped some tea, then gasped a deep breath. "At least the earl has offered to do the honorable thing to save your reputation. That's the sign of a true gentleman."

"He cares nothing for me. And I feel nothing for him. How could I? I don't want to marry that cold-hearted stranger!" Allegra fought against her rising tears, remembering the stony silence she'd endured in the coach from Hungerford to London. The earl had dozed and brooded in his corner, refusing to speak with her. "I didn't run away just to fall into another matrimonial trap."

"Oh, dear, oh, dear. You always were a high-spirited girl, and now that you're a young lady, well, one expects your mama to take better care of you."

"Like I told you, Mother has only Pinkney's best interests at heart. She would like to see me gone from Temple Manor, since I can't abide him. The tension has been steadily mounting ever since he moved in. I know Pinkney has been feathering his nest with Mama's money. There's nothing I can do about that. Oh, Auntie, I've been so lonely without Giles to bolster my flagging spirits."

"Well, I suppose your harum-scarum brother adores you, but he isn't suitable company now that you're a grown woman. He always embroiled you in his wild schemes, if I recall correctly."

"Except for the servants, I had no friends at Temple Manor when Giles left for Oxford."

Irene patted her hand, and Allegra almost burst into tears, but she refused to let weakness overcome her.

Her aunt said, "I don't want to delve into the wrongs of your past, but your mother always was an indifferent parent. She let her unhappiness with your father poison her relationship with you and Giles."

"I shall write to Giles immediately. I'll ask him to come here rather than travel to Wiltshire at the end of term." Allegra gave her aunt a searching glance. "You don't mind if I stay for a while?"

"Of course not! You know you're always welcome here." She wrinkled her brow. "But what are we going to say to Pinkney and your mother? They'll be in a rare taking once they hear about your adventure with Lord Wyndham."

"I don't know," Allegra said, feeling small and inexperienced. She should be excited to be in the Metropolis for the second time in her life. Her first visit had coincided with her seventh birthday, and she didn't remember much of that occasion.

"You shouldn't have to marry Ezra Skelton," said Irene with much vehemence, "but your stepfather is your guardian. Pinkney has the right to pull you back to Wiltshire without ado and tie you to Skelton." She leaned forward and offered her niece a sugared pastry from a silver plate.

"I won't go."

"You must eat and gather you strength, my dear. Your problems won't look as insurmountable once your stomach is filled."

Allegra tried to smile, but the effort was too great. Her heart sat stonelike in her chest.

"Is it true that I'm ruined, as Lord Wyndham said?"

Irene pursed her lips. "That, dear Allegra, is the bitter truth. You won't be able to hold up your head in this town if we cannot devise a suitable explanation why you were in the earl's company at dawn, unchaperoned."

"He said he would call here when he'd recovered from the grippe."

"Well," Irene said with a reassuring smile, "we had better hurry up, then."

chapter 3

*T*rue to his word, the Earl of Wyndham delivered his card at Half Moon Street exactly one week after his first encounter with Miss Temple. His limbs still quivered with weakness, but at least he'd come through the ravishing fever with his life intact. Morose, he kicked his heels in the front parlor while the butler bore his card upstairs upon a silver salver. The black kitten with the ridiculous name of "Beau" sat on the mantelpiece glaring at him and swishing its tail. The feline had grown in the past week and looked quite at home, lord of the manor in fact. The dashed creature had brought misfortune like a bad wind into his life....

Wyndham remembered his recent encounter with Miss Temple as if it had been a nightmare brought on by the fever. He recalled that she'd been pretty enough with soft chestnut hair and incredibly blue eyes, but her loveliness did not endear her to him. Female beauty made him cautious. A cruel heart usually lurked beneath the lushest beauty; he knew that from experience.

Miss Temple had looked like a frightened rabbit, and as innocent, he recalled. That was the reason he'd felt forced to present himself at Half Moon Street. His conscience would never rest if he didn't renew his offer of protection.

Nevertheless, the prospect filled his heart with ice. How could he have been so addle-brained as to land himself in this awkward situation?

Mrs. Irene Sinclair swept into the salon dressed in a plain, pale blue morning gown and a frilly cap. Short of stature, she nevertheless gave an impression of imperiousness. Instead of wearing a haughty expression, however, she wore a kind smile for him. "Lord Wyndham, I'm so grateful that you took the pains to pay me a visit."

Ian bowed over the outstretched hand. "Madam, I would not shirk my duty. How is Miss Temple? I gather she is still with you?"

Irene sat down on a Chippendale chair and motioned him toward an identical chair on the other side of a bow-legged table. "She's still here. I have written to her mother and stepfather in Wiltshire. I surmise 'twill be only a matter of hours before they descend upon London. They would have traveled up earlier, but Mr. Pinkney took ill with a stomach ailment. Mrs. Pinkney would not travel up alone—does not worry unduly—" Irene clamped her lips shut and clasped her sturdy hands in her lap. She gazed at him intently. "You must understand that Allegra is the sweetest lady alive. She would never scheme and plot to foist herself upon you in a vulnerable moment." She paused, waiting for a reply that he did not offer. "I heard you had the grippe. I pray you are fully recovered."

Wyndham nodded, still feeling quite weak. He'd planned to put this lady in her place if necessary, if she'd decided to throw a temper tantrum. Her kindness threw him off-keel. "Yes, I'm fit as a fiddle, thank you."

"Can I offer you some refreshment—a glass of port perhaps?"

The earl shook his head. "No. I came in all haste—concerned with Miss Temple's reputation." Better broach the subject quickly and get it over with. However much he'd twisted and turned the problem in his mind during the last sennight, he could only come up with one solution. He would have to marry the girl. "I have worried a great deal."

"That sentiment does you credit, my lord. I have fretted, too. I'm sure however, that Miss Temple won't allow you to inconvenience yourself on her behalf. She would have found a way to travel into London even if your coach hadn't happened to pull in for a change of horses at the inn where she was hiding." Irene wafted her hand in front of her face as if finding the room too hot. "Not that I approve of her actions, mind you. She's much too high-spirited, always was. From what I've heard by letter, her stepfather is in a rare taking. Allegra refuses to comply with his plans. I *do* understand her reluctance to wed a man fifty years her senior. Ezra Skelton is a man known for his ... er, unsavory liaisons."

Wyndham wrinkled his brow in thought. "Her stepfather does not seem to have Miss Temple's best interests at heart."

"You might say that, my lord," Irene said darkly. "It's likely Mr. Pinkney—the stepfather—sees a way to line his own pockets through Skelton. His land marches with that of Temple Manor. I must confess, I'm terribly concerned and wish that my niece did not have to be forced into matrimony."

On that dire note the door opened and Miss Temple entered. The earl stood and could not but stare at her. Dressed in a high-waisted canary-yellow gown with a frill around the neck, she didn't carry the air of a frightened rabbit any longer. Still, a shadow of apprehension clouded her deep blue eyes as she looked at him. Her face held a quality of stubborn determination despite her youthful age. Even though a strong character was clearly emerging, she had a vulnerable, hesitant air as if unsure how to proceed.

That vulnerability touched his heart just like the innocence of a newborn foal or puppy would. He couldn't be angry with her even though he felt he'd been wronged.

"Come in, Allegra. Your benefactor has arrived to pay his respects."

"I hope you're feeling much better," Allegra said in a soft, melodious voice.

"My health is much improved, thank you." Despite being flawed with the traits of a hoyden who dared to barge into strange coaches at dawn, she was pleasing to the eye in a soft feminine way.

He wished she'd entered the room with a smile instead of that veil of apprehension on her face. It was clear by the fear in her eyes that she expected him to lash out at her—or do something worse. Was the thought of marriage to him so distasteful? Wyndham pondered this novel idea.

Staring at him, she remained by the door as if poised for flight. The kitten gamboled across the room, and she lifted it into her arms, holding it like a shield against the world. For the second time in his acquaintance with the kitten, he felt an inexplicable urge to wring its scrawny neck.

Allegra's hope sank to the soles of her kid slippers. This worldly gentleman—dressed at the very peak of elegance in a coat of brown cloth, pale buff pantaloons, a yellow striped waistcoat, faultless neckcloth, and Hessians so polished she could have used them for a mirror—had not an ounce of feeling for her.

When not tortured by a fever, his silver-blue eyes were calm and penetrating, knowing, mature. The dark smudges still remained under his eyes, but he looked fit, tall, powerful, and ever so intimidating. *God, give me strength,* she prayed silently.

Quailing, she stepped toward the middle of the room. "Is this the first day you've ventured outside, milord?"

"You're correct on that score," he replied. "It is a lovely

day for a walk." She could detect no emotion in that statement, and she worried what would come next.

"Surely there was no need to pay us a visit," she began, "I meant to—"

"No need?" he asked, his lips quirking upward. She remembered that cynical smile from their first encounter in the coach. "I'd say there's every need, Miss Temple. By now that busybody Mrs. Fishwood will have revealed the whole—with a great deal of relish, I wager—to any number of cronies who care to listen. London will be buzzing with rumors soon if it isn't already. I don't know, as I have yet to visit my club."

"I don't see any reason to listen to the tattlemongers," Allegra said stiffly.

He remained standing, one arm behind him, and one braced on the back of the Chippendale chair. "Perhaps you don't care a jot about your reputation, Miss Temple, but I care about *mine*."

"Of course you do, my lord," inserted Irene hastily. "Anyone must see that the encounter with Mrs. Fishwood and Mrs. Drummond-Burrell has put you in an awful dilemma."

He straightened his already straight back. "That's true, but I'm not in the habit of avoiding problems or shirking my duty, Mrs. Sinclair."

An ominous silence hung in the room, and Allegra dreaded his next words.

"I've come to renew my offer for Miss Temple," he continued. "It's the only way to restore her reputation, and mine."

"But—" began Irene.

"I know you can't give your permission, Mrs. Sinclair, but before I approach the irate Mr. Pinkney, I would like to know if Miss Temple has fully understood the issue. I need her cooperation." He leveled his gaze on her, and

Allegra took a step back. His eyes were cold, as freezing as a January day.

"I daresay it's very handsome of you, Lord Wyndham," Irene said, "but I'm not sure—"

"I know this is a highly irregular way to approach the issue of marriage, but I would like to hear Miss Temple speak her mind," the earl went on, still pinning his hard gaze on Allegra. "I want to hear her say that she understands there is no other way."

"I ... I'm very flattered by the offer, naturally," Allegra and averted her gaze. "I don't see, however, how our nuptials will solve anything." Her voice started trembling. "You don't care a fig for me, and I ... and I—" *loathe you*, she added silently.

He shrugged. "I believe it's a mutual sentiment, then, but that shouldn't stop us from marriage. Sooner or later I would've had to face the possibility of getting shackled. Now is as good a time as any."

"This is preposterous!" Allegra gathered all her courage and clutched the purring kitten to her chest. "You speak about marriage as if it were equal to purchasing a horse at Tattersall's. How can you treat the subject in such a callous fashion?" Her voice rose a notch. "In fact, I believe you must show more feeling when choosing a dashed horse!"

"Allegra!" Aunt Irene cried.

"I don't see that there is much difference between purchasing a new team or choosing a wife," he said imperturbably. "In a way I'm relieved that the choice has been taken from my hands. I'm sure we'll deal tolerably well together."

Allegra glanced at her aunt and read the dread in the older woman's eyes. Keeping her focus on Irene, she said, "Surely marriage should be based on ... on love." She recalled that Aunt Irene had wed for love with Aurelius

Sinclair, who had died in a coaching accident five years before.

Irene bowed her head and closed her eyes as if reluctant to look at her niece. Allegra knew she had touched the heart of the matter.

"I don't like to repeat myself. Love is not important," the odious earl replied.

Allegra kept staring at her aunt. "Tell him, Auntie, tell him."

Irene lifted her blue gaze and viewed the portrait of Aurelius hanging above the mantelpiece. "I daresay love is significant, but in this case, your reputation is more important, Allegra. With your reputation in ruins, no one will marry you, not even Ezra Skelton. I daresay you must accept the earl's generous offer."

Flames of anger flared hotly in Allegra's heart. "You are a fool, Aunt Irene, and so are you," she added, turning to the earl. "I don't care what people think of me."

"You will, when everyone ignores you in the street and the gentlemen refuse to dance with you at the balls. That is, *if* you manage to get any invitations. I doubt that after the scandal reaches every ear in town." The earl spoke matter-of-factly, and Allegra felt very young and insignificant.

"There's no other choice. You must state that you're willing to marry me. Then I shall take up the matter with Mr. Pinkney." His lips widened in that cynical smile again. "I'm certain he won't have any objection—not by the time I'm finished. I shall tell him a few truths about his lax chaperonage."

Allegra took a deep breath. "Do I have a choice?"

He shook his head.

"Again, I must say it's a most generous offer," said Irene. "Allegra could not expect to make such an advantageous marriage."

"Perhaps we can endeavor to make it the wedding of the year," the earl said sarcastically. He stepped over to Allegra and held out his hand. She backed away, shaking her head. Her mind reeled with the suggestion he had put forward. His very purposeful pursuit of her bowled her over. His lack of emotion chilled her, and she sought for a way to save herself. For once Aunt Irene wasn't supporting her but played the society game with this cold stranger. If the polite circles of London could so easily turn their backs on her, then by God, they weren't worth a groat.

She would make her own circle of friends, just like she had at Temple Manor! The maids and the grooms all were her cronies, and they didn't look down their noses when she appeared in her oldest gown at the stables, or went down on her knees to weed the flower borders. The very thought of the Earl of Wyndham going down on his knees to weed a border was too ridiculous even to contemplate. Nor would Aunt Irene muddy her fashionable gowns with soil.

London appeared so very different from the country, and she realized that she was naive for believing that she could save herself. The future loomed excessively bleak, and the blame was all her own.

"I suppose my true opinion holds little power," she said as the earl headed for the door.

The earl halted on the threshold. "Your father would have approved of this union." He addressed Irene. "I expect you to explain matters further to your niece. It's evident that she has no notion of how to go on in Society." He leveled an inscrutable glance at Allegra. "Our wedding day shall be exactly one month from today."

chapter 4

It rained on Allegra's wedding day, literally poured, the water ruining silk flowers on hats and washing the starch out of the gentlemen's neckcloths and shirt points. The hundred wedding guests in St. George's, Hanover Square, looked like an assortment of high-bred birds whose glorious plumage had been sadly mauled by the elements.

Allegra's pink roses drooped just as her heart wilted in her chest. After four weeks of pleading with her aunt to find another solution than a marriage of convenience, Allegra now stood next to the tall and powerful Earl of Wyndham by the altar.

Nothing could persuade him into changing his mind about wedding her. Early on, she had discovered that when her husband-to-be decided on something, he set to work accomplishing his goal with exceptional single-mindedness.

The earl, accompanied by Allegra and her aunt, had on the day of their interview at Irene's town house gone to confront Woodruff Pinkney at Grillon's hotel. Allegra's head still rang from the admonitions her stepfather had poured over her. Pinkney's burly body had towered over her, his lizardlike eyes boring into her as if eager to skewer her heart.

"I cannot stress enough, Stepdaughter, how you humiliated your Mother and Myself with your Shameless Flight. It is inconceivable how you could bring such Disgrace to your family! Your mother cannot hold her head up in Chippenham, and the Fault lies wholly at your feet. I had your future—a brilliant one—planned to the last detail, and you showed your disdain in the most Brazen way imaginable."

He'd pursed his fleshy lips and thrown an acid glance in the earl's direction. "Ezra Skelton would have served you well as a husband, and you would have honored your family when Abiding by my choice."

One thing Allegra had learned: Pinkney did not like anyone acquiring a more elevated social position than himself. He would sever friendships for less, and Allegra hoped he would be reluctant to speak with her once she'd become the Countess of Wyndham.

"I'm sorry, Stepfather, yet if I understand you correctly, a match with Lord Wyndham appears more advantageous than one with that greedy prune of a man, Mr. Skelton."

"Allegra!" Aunt Irene admonished.

"I am Shocked at your choice in words," Pinkney had thundered. "I expect a show of Reverence for the absent Mr. Skelton."

The earl had smiled his odd smile, but when Allegra had given him a searching glance, he'd only raised his eyebrows in an infuriatingly noncommittal way.

She had given her mother a glance, pleading for support, but her parent had only waved a lethargic hand. "Your steppapa knows best, Allegra," she'd said with a yawn. "You should listen to him and obey, but honestly, I don't care whom you wed." Mrs. Pinkney had given a bloodless smile, plunging Allegra into a pit of loneliness. Only Irene had truly lent her support, squeezing her hand and draping a comforting arm around her shoulders.

As Allegra found out that Ezra Skelton had cried off in the wake of her disgrace, she knew she had only one choice, to wed the intimidating Earl of Wyndham. In other words, there really hadn't been a choice at all—as he'd so easily pointed out earlier in the day.

The earl might be cold-hearted, but he was not burdened with years and was not an eyesore. She would live far away from her odious stepfather, which was a great advantage, and to battle any feeling of loneliness, she would invite Giles to visit her in London.

"The only way to restore your daughter's reputation is by a speedy marriage. I've already offered a settlement—a very favorable one, I might add—for her hand," Wyndham had said, concluding the argument most forcefully.

Just with such forcefulness, the earl had claimed her and borne her to the altar of St. George's.

When she now glanced at his glacial profile, she wanted to burst into tears. The man had not one ounce of feeling in his hardened heart.

The only bright spot in the torturous procedure was that dear Giles had come down from Oxford to lend his moral support for the day.

"You've really kicked up a lark this time, sis," he'd said earlier this morning. "What in the world induced you to take up with the Earl of Wyndham? Much too high in the instep for the likes of us. You'll be bored to flinders with such an exacting husband."

She'd observed her brother's carefree grin and new style of ridiculously high shirt points, extravagant neckcloth, and garish waistcoat of pink and blue stripes. "I shall prevail somehow, find ways to entertain myself," she'd replied, but inside she had quaked, and she still did.

She heard the wind of whispers behind her as she stumbled through her vows. Then her bridegroom gripped her hand firmly and pushed a golden band adorned with a large ruby onto her finger, burdening it with unaccustomed weight.

The earl's hard mouth descended on hers for a perfunctory peck. He smelled pleasantly of peppermint, and if she hadn't been *victimized* in this manner, she might have found the earl a highly personable man. His silvery gaze probed hers for a moment, trying to read her thoughts, trying to decipher her emotions. She swallowed the lump in her throat, but it wouldn't go down, and her heart fluttered most uncomfortably.

From the lips of her aunt, she'd heard the tale of his broken heart. Everybody in London seemed to know that Justine Bryerly had broken off her engagement to the earl. The rumor flying around the Capital ever since the announcement of Allegra's betrothal to Wyndham had been inserted in the *Gazette* said that the earl was marrying to spite his erstwhile fiancée.

The salacious gossip had caught like wildfire and was broached in every drawing room, mortifying Allegra more than the earl's callous proposal had.

How cruel were the gossipmongers, and how inflexible their minds! When Allegra, with a trembling heart, dared to bring up the subject with Wyndham in the carriage that bore them away from St. George's, he only shrugged and said, "You shouldn't listen to gossip."

"I don't." She tried to control her trembling voice. "But this is more than gossip, isn't it?"

His already stern face hardened, and his lips thinned. "Let me clarify the facts. Not too long ago, I was betrothed to Miss Bryerly. She jilted me, and that was the end of it. Are you going to nag me about her?" He laughed mirthlessly. "That, my dear Allegra, hints at jealousy. No need for that, surely. Ours is a union of convenience, and we both know how this all came about."

"I do not nag, nor am I jealous," she had replied in a

rare show of icy pride. Usually, she was good at standing up for herself, but the earl daunted her more than any other gentleman she had known. She barely dared to open her mouth.

Perhaps he hated her, she thought as she stole a glance at his closed face. *After all, I forced him into this situation with my thoughtless action.*

She would have been relieved had she been able to read Wyndham's thoughts. He held no antipathy in his heart; he always stood by his decisions. He admitted to a certain disappointment that the bride wasn't Justine, but couldn't bear a grudge toward the innocent woman beside him. Besides, he understood that she hadn't schemed to get into his coach that fateful night which decided his future. If he hadn't been so sick, this would never have come to pass. He would have put her on a stagecoach, or delivered her to her parents' doorstep. Perhaps Fate had a hand in choosing his bride.... There was no denying that *something* had meddled in their lives.

Like most couples who married for convenience, they would find a way to rub along. It was high time he set up his nursery, and his bride came of good country stock. Once an heir had been born, they would lead separate lives.

He gave her a sideways glance, noticing the near panic darkening her eyes and the trembling of her soft lips. This was not a happy day for her, either, but she would have to adapt herself to her new life.

He tried to gauge how she would welcome him on their wedding night. Most likely she wouldn't be prepared—be skittish as a colt. He would have to go patiently with her, or make an enemy for life.

She looked lovely in a white lace-trimmed gown and a frivolous embroidered veil framing her sweet face. That innocent face and fearful eyes spoke to his more gallant feelings, more so than her defiant tongue. He'd done the right thing marrying the chit. It was to her advantage to stay away from that dreadful Woodruff Pinkney and his indolent wife. He hoped Allegra hadn't taken after her mother, but her honorable father, Sir Edwin.

"Did you know, my dear," he said as the coach rumbled toward the Wyndham mansion in Berkley Square where the wedding breakfast would be held, "that my father applied the advice on grains that Sir Edwin provided to his acres?"

Allegra shook her head. "No, I had no idea."

Rain pelted viciously against the roof, and Wyndham wondered if it was a prophecy of a stormy future.

"The old earl always tried to improve the crops at our country estate, High Wyndham," he continued. "Fact is, my parent rarely came to London. He was a country squire at heart. I know that he discussed crops for hours with anyone interested in his plans."

Allegra smiled fondly as she recalled Sir Edwin. "Father knew all there was about rotating crops and refining the grains."

"Quite the scholar, eh?" Wyndham said, making the effort to lighten the funereal mood in the coach. "Is your brother Giles cut from that same cloth?"

Allegra's tight expression transformed into a wide smile, dazzling Wyndham with its brightness. His heart made an odd sort of jump in his chest, and his breath caught momentarily.

"Oh, no, my brother has no head for books. He could probably take a degree in ale tasting, though. He's quite the connoisseur. Knows his whiskey, too."

"Hmm, I daresay he knows his card games as well, like any 'well-educated' young blood."

"I should imagine so," Allegra said, blushing, and fidgeted with the posy of pink roses in her hand. "Giles is the most kind-hearted man imaginable, but he's somewhat reckless."

"You have a streak of that as well, but I wager you don't know much about whiskey and card games." Wyndham was gratified to see the sadness completely leave her eyes. The sparkle of humor suited her so much better.

"I most certainly do not," she said. "I had a governess until I turned fifteen, a music teacher, and a painting master. Then I went to an academy for young ladies in Bath for six months."

"Yes ... how uncouth of me, I completely forgot to ask you about your accomplishments."

"You were in a hurry to get a wife, *any* wife," she said pointedly. "My achievements were of little importance."

"I suppose my indifference hurts your pride."

"Indifference?" Her lovely blue eyes flashed. "My lord, what you have shown me is beyond that. You wouldn't care if I were squint-eyed and possessing only one leg."

He chuckled. "That's a gross exaggeration, Allegra. I do care."

"I suppose it wouldn't be seemly to bring squint-eyed children to bear the Wyndham name, but you were in such haste to marry. You have only yourself to blame." Allegra knew she sounded waspish, but she was beyond caring. Her nerves had been sorely taxed this morning under the curious, and pitying, gazes of Wyndham's friends at church.

He shrugged, and the warmth he'd felt momentarily in his heart disappeared. His chest felt as dead and empty as a desert. "I seem to recall that I rescued a certain reckless maiden from unequivocal ruination. Doesn't that count for something?"

Allegra blushed, the pink in her cheeks rivaling the hue

of the roses in her hand. "I don't know. Perhaps ruination would have been better than this charade." A veil of caution fell over her eyes as she raised her face toward his. "I had expected that marriage would follow a mutual love declaration, but I must be sadly deluded."

"Is that what you want? A love declaration? I can easily give you one."

"You speak with flippancy! You are a cold man."

"I have been accused of worse."

Damn it, he swore silently. He wasn't handling the situation right, but he couldn't very well go down on his knee and profess his love when he didn't feel any. He couldn't lie; it wasn't in his character to pretend.

"I think you look lovely, and that's the truth," he began, thinking of himself as a blind man who fumbled along a strange wall.

Her soft mouth pursed as if she was considering his words. "Thank you," she said at last in a stiff voice. "You look rather handsome yourself."

For a moment the faint blush on her cheeks and her cautious words eased the emptiness in his heart. He felt ridiculously pleased with himself that he'd found a way to bridge the threatening chasm between them.

The coach halted in front of the Wyndham mansion, and footmen were running down the wide front steps holding up umbrellas against the pelting rain. His heart sank at the thought of entering the house that held so many sad memories and such deadening loneliness. Every time he looked at the white imperious facade, so grand, and so impersonal, the same sinking feeling went though his stomach. It always had, as long as he could remember.

"We are here. The guests will arrive shortly," the earl said in a more abrupt voice than he intended.

He helped her down, and protected from the rain, she walked up the steps to the entrance. The butler, sporting dandelion tufts of white hair, and black beady eyes in a bloodhound's face, bowed stiffly in the door opening. A lackey stood statuelike beside him, and another at the base of the curving interior staircase.

To her surprise, the earl scooped her up into his arms and carried her over the threshold into the brightly lit hallway. His muscular arms held her slender body as easily as if it weighed no more than a walking cane. She could not help but be aware of his close proximity, the fresh scent of his newly laundered linen, the warmth of his breath on her cheek, the sheer strength of him. He still daunted her with his commanding presence, but she could sense no animosity from him. Perhaps only a slight tension, as if he were holding his breath.

He set her down, and her legs wobbled as she looked into his silvery-blue eyes. She could have sworn they pierced right through her, baring her soul, making her weak-kneed. Flustered, she tore her gaze away and followed her temporary maid, commandeered from the kitchen staff until she could hire someone, upstairs to refresh herself.

The first guest to arrive was Wyndham's cousin and heir, the Honorable Percival Harcombe. A pink of the *ton*, he sauntered into the mansion, his soft body resplendent in a royal blue cutaway silk coat, black inexpressibles, and a stunning waistcoat patterned with large white fleurs-de-lis on a green background. The silver buttons were big and shiny enough to use as mirrors, Allegra thought as she greeted him with a smile.

"First-rate wedding, m'dear," he said and pecked the air above her hand. "Splendid do!"

Abashed, she gazed at this bright tulip, noticing only the kindness in his pale blue eyes and the dimple in his apple-plump chin. "Welcome," she said. "I pray that you'll consider me your friend, Mr. Harcombe."

He tweaked her fingertips and made an elegant leg. "You must call me Percy, m'dear. It won't do to stand upon formalities. Not now as we are family. Pea and pod, y'know." He threw a quick glance at the earl beside her. "Or pea and pod might be a mite too close if Wyndham's icy glare is any indication." He nodded in the earl's direction and delivered the next sally. "Not to worry, however. My visits will be of the wholly innocent variety. As that great lummox already knows, I do make a nuisance of myself in this house. Wyndham has a superb cook who knows how to appease my delicate constitution."

"One of these days, you'll eat me out of my own house, Perce," the earl muttered. "I shall be reduced to begging on the streets."

Percy waved a careless plump hand and studied Allegra's face appreciatively. "If you need my assistance to subdue this great boar, just send around a message. Lodgings in St. James's—Jermyn Street. I shall set him on the straight and narrow." He glanced around the hallway critically. "I daresay nothing changes around here. The same gloomy walls, the same forbidding portraits of the same dull lot of Wyndhams. I think you might redecorate this monstrous house soon, m'dear. I shall be delighted to give you my advice on the color scheme as I have quite the reputation for a bold vision and an unerring eye."

"If anything, you certainly have *boldness* at heart, and no lack of confidence," the earl said ruefully. "And a decidedly slippery tongue."

Allegra eyed Percy's splendid attire and wondered about the fashionable formulation of taste. "I shall certainly remember your offer," she said, hard put to suppress a laugh.

"Don't you worry, m'dear. I shall take you under my wing," Percy added absentmindedly as he peered through his quizzing glass at the slightly faded tapestry on the wall. "Shameful decor, this is. A disgrace." He patted the ancient material, waved languidly, and went in search of the buffet.

The earl snorted beside Allegra. "I take it Perce has now put you in mind of turning my house upside down and flinging the furniture out the window."

Allegra glanced at him to see if his face displayed anger, but she saw only wry amusement. It had not occurred to her to suggest anything as forward as redecorating the Berkley Square mansion, but she gathered her wits and replied carelessly, "I have given it some thought, but I wouldn't—"

"Just don't touch the library. I've spent tedious hours setting it up the way I like it."

She gazed at him in wonder. "You wouldn't *mind* some changes, then?"

He shrugged, his expression bland. "You are now the mistress of the house. This mausoleum has not seen the caring hand of a woman since my mother went to her just rewards eight and twenty years ago."

"Eight and twenty . . . years? Then no one told you stories at bedtime or . . . or hugged you?" Allegra could easily picture his bleak childhood directed by stern tutors and servants in vast mansions.

His lips twisted sideways, and a muscle bunched in his jaw. "Perhaps a childhood not so unlike your own?"

"Mother might not have cared, but I had a nanny with an extravagant imagination and a warm heart, and my father told adventurous tales about creatures in foreign lands before bedtime."

"An enviable situation, I'm sure," he said coolly.

"What about the old earl? What did he like besides farming? Did he remarry?" she hastened to ask just as more carriages pulled up in front of the mansion. To her surprise, she experienced a deep need to discover more about her aloof husband.

"He had no time for striplings in short coats, but I perceived him as an interesting person, a man full of zeal. As a dedicated farmer he doubled the yield of the Wyndham estates. He never remarried, too principled for that. I know he was a lonely man at heart, sorely missed my mother. Revered her memory." He gave Allegra a hard stare. "Some say I took her life at birth, too big of a burden for her delicate body. I don't know. Father never said anything about it."

Nor did he absolve you of the blame, Allegra thought as she sensed his loneliness like a faint echoing coldness in the air. So many years he'd lived in the vastness of his inheritance and the indifferent heart of his family. "I'm surprised he didn't remarry to give you brothers and sisters."

"Father was married to the land. I've always had Perce, of course. We grew up together, inseparable, however unlikely that might seem—in view of our current contrasting personalities and tastes."

Allegra looked at his elegant, if subdued, accouterments. A series of intricate folds comprised his starched neckcloth, but those were the only extravagance she could detect. He didn't wear a single seal or fob, only his signet ring. To her, he appeared vastly more attractive than his flamboyant cousin.

"I'm sure Beau Brummell, were he still in London, would have disapproved of your cousin's taste in waistcoats," she said, hiding a smile behind her hand, as she remembered that notorious arbiter of fashion who had fled to the Continent to evade his debtors. She found that she enjoyed conversing with her husband, their exchange giving her the same warm feeling she felt when discovering a new friend.

"Tolerance was not one of Brummell's character traits." The earl gave her a searching glance as if measuring the depth of her knowledge of the world. "At the moment, he's probably cutting some hapless Frogs with his scathing tongue."

She laughed and noted the faint smile on his lips. "The Regent surely does not miss his erstwhile friend," she said, desperately wanting to show Wyndham that she wasn't an ignorant country yokel. "They ended up enemies." Despising herself for her need to impress him, she looked away.

"A sterling friend is hard to come by," he said with a meaningful lift of the eyebrows. "The closest people sometimes betray your trust. I can't abide liars and cheats."

The guests saved her from the intensity of her husband's gaze. Did he fear she would become his enemy? It was clear he didn't know her well enough to recognize her deep sense of loyalty to the persons who touched her heart.

"Lady Wyndham!" a plump matron exclaimed and enveloped Allegra in a perfumed embrace. Allegra fought to subdue a sneeze, and the lady nudged the earl in the arm. "You're a lucky man, Wyndham! Your countess is sweetness personified, don't you think?"

He smiled politely, and Allegra searched for some warmth in his expression. *The Countess of Wyndham.* The title—her new name—sounded foreign, as if attached to some lofty, older stranger. *Lady Wyndham.*

"I hope that we'll become prodigiously good friends," the matron gushed, and Allegra could not find a suitable answer as she pondered her new—very elevated—status.

Mrs. Lucrezia Fishwood was one of the first guests to arrive. She gave Allegra her fingertips to shake and a measuring stare through her quizzing glass. "I daresay you knew precisely to a pin how to nab a wealthy husband, Allegra," she said with a frozen smile. "Looking at you, a simple country maiden, I would never have thought you capable of such brazen forwardness."

Allegra shrunk under the censuring words.

The earl leaned forward and murmured, "I suppose the leading ladies of Chippenham inspire such impudent behavior in the young. Where else would they learn it?"

Mrs. Fishwood's mouth fell open, and her head snapped back. "I say!" With a ruffled frown she walked with a regal tilt to her nose into the drawing room.

Allegra gave the earl a grateful smile. She wished he would return her smile, but he stared right past her. "Thank you."

"Don't mention it."

The rest of the guests welled into the house, filling it with chatter and high-pitched laughter. All the forced smiles and useless conversations gave Allegra a headache, and by the end of the day, as the last lingering guest left, she was ready to collapse onto the nearest sofa.

The earl had gone in search of his own rooms, and Allegra drew a sigh of relief. The most trying day of her life had died into this—a great stillness among the chaos of trays holding dirty glasses, plates, and cake crumbs. Servants moved ghostlike in and out of the room.

Her mother and stepfather had returned to Grillon's, where they'd spent the last two days. They planned to return to Chippenham on the morrow. Giles, her ally, had gone back to Oxford right after the ceremony. She wished he could have remained to lend his moral support, but his cronies beckoned from afar.

Dispirited and apprehensive about the night to come, Allegra fought down an urge to run away, preferably to Aunt Irene's town house in Half Moon Street. Irene had been a rock ever since that disastrous day when the earl informed her that Allegra was to become his wife—no matter what objection anyone might raise. That day seemed lifetimes ago.

Allegra was a different person now, all childish notions

dead and gone from the day when Stepfather demanded that she marry Ezra Skelton. In her wildest dreams she had never thought that she would be part—or instigator—of the series of events that had led her to this night.

Filled with apprehension, she went upstairs to her boudoir. On the morrow she would travel with Wyndham to Yorkshire to spend the honeymoon at a distant relative's estate. If only it was over and done with! What would she say to the earl every day for a whole week? Her tongue would tie itself into a knot, and her brain would lose all intelligent thought. A whole *week* in his presence!

With a heavy heart Allegra entered her bedchamber. Beau bounced off the bed and came to wind his sinewy body around her legs. She scooped him up into her arms.

"Ye're cold as a gravestone, melady," said Lucy, the kitchen maid, as she helped her mistress take off the elaborate satin wedding gown. "It be hot as th' divil's backside outdoors, hot for a spring night, that is," the intrepid maid continued in her monotone voice, then clapped her hand to her mouth.

Stifling a startled laugh, Allegra sat down by the dressing table and stared at Lucy. She'd never encountered a servant—except for the stable grooms—with such a coarse tongue.

"Are you London born, Lucy?" Allegra asked to still her curiosity and curb her mirth.

Lucy nodded, then whispered. "I'm not supposed to open me mouth in yer presence, milady. Dogwood said ye'd be that shocked. 'E'll flay the skin off me back."

"I'm somewhat surprised that such torture still exists in England," Allegra said dryly.

"Cook says I talk the 'ind leg off a donkey. Cor, 'tis but God's truth. I'm 'ard put to shut me gob." Lucy, tall and strong, leaned over Allegra's shoulder. She grasped a brush and began brushing her mistress's hair. "Dogwood be me third uncle's fourth cousin, and 'e recommended me to th' master when no abigail could be 'ired in time. Said I could arrange 'air fancylike. Y'see, 'Is Lordship trusts Dogwood, so 'ere I am, until ye find a real maid, the sort wot takes on genteel airs and tilts 'er nose 'eavenward."

"Where did you learn to dress hair?" Allegra asked, amused by the outspoken Lucy. She quite liked the soothing brush strokes.

"I used to do for the actresses at Drury Lane, I did. I laundered their things, as well. I sews as neat a stitch as Mrs. Buxton, the 'ousekeeper.' "

Allegra held back an exclamation of surprise and fought her urge to laugh. "Actresses? Does His Lordship know about this?"

Lucy gave her a long look in the mirror. "No, melady, lest ye, yerself, tells 'im."

Allegra was inclined to trust the worthy Dogwood's judgment. She'd already gleaned that not much passed the butler's eagle eye—despite his rigid expression. If he trusted Lucy, then she would, too, despite Lucy's more than colorful language.

"We'll get ye ready fer bed in a jiffy, melady." Lucy gave a broad smile and a wink. Allegra stiffened.

"Th—there's no hurry . . . surely," she said lamely. "In fact, I'd like you to brush my hair two hundred strokes tonight."

"Can't count that far, melady." Lucy nodded sagely. "I understand. Ye want to look yer best for 'Is Lordship. 'E'll be bangin' on yer door presently."

Allegra's hands flew to her face, and she watched in the mirror as a crimson flush washed over her cheeks.

Lucy's pale blue eyes widened knowingly, and a mousy brown curl bobbed under the rim of her voluminous white cap. "Ye be afraid, melady, bain't ye?"

Allegra dropped her gaze to the wedding ring on her

finger. New obligations weighed on her shoulders, obligations she knew nothing about. She wished Aunt Irene had told her about the secrets of marriage, but there simply hadn't been time between the fittings of the trousseau.

"Don't ye worry. 'Is Lordship bain't no ogre. A manly feller. 'E'll service ye with great style, I'll wager."

"Service me?" Allegra asked in dying tones. A tremble of fear went through her.

"Ye're from the country, ain't ye? You've seen th' bulls service th' cows. It be the same thing. Ye just 'aveta be willin' and eager. Spread wide, like."

Allegra gasped in agitation. She had no idea what Lucy was talking about, but surely the maid had widely overstepped her bounds. She rose on quivering legs. "I think I will retire now, Lucy. Help me with the nightgown, then you can go to bed. I won't need you again tonight."

Lucy grinned. "That's the right spirit, melady. 'Twill please 'Is Lordship no end t' find ye full o' pluck, ready and waitin'."

Allegra flinched at the blunt words. Lucy tweaked the gossamer nightgown of gauze and lace in place, then left—slamming the door to announce her departure, no doubt, Allegra thought darkly.

Feeling naked and depressed, she shook as if she had a fit of the ague. Huddling under the down cover, she pinned her burning gaze to the door that separated her husband's bedchamber from her own.

chapter 5

Allegra jumped with fright as a knock came five minutes later. Her heart lurched and she could not find her voice to ask the earl to enter. He entered anyway and closed the door softly behind him.

Allegra slid farther under the cover, praying the mattress would open up and devour her. To keep an eye on him, she peeped over the edge of the monogrammed sheet. He looked handsome in a relaxed way, dark hair tousled, no stiff neckcloth at his neck, only bare skin.... Allegra turned to a pillar of ice as she realized that he wore *nothing* underneath the loosely belted silk dressing gown patterned with an Oriental motif of birds and branches. She observed the strong column of his neck, her gaze traveling downward to the bare muscular chest, which was covered with whorls of dark hair.

She gasped and squeezed her eyes shut. If only he would go away! *Oh, dear!*

"Good evening, Allegra," the earl said, his deep voice carrying a hint of humor.

She counted his steps as he came closer. Two more and he would be right by the bed. One ... two ... *Doom.* The mattress moved as he sat down beside her and tugged at the sheet that she gripped so convulsively.

"Lost your voice?" he chided.

She had to look at him, eminently aware of the dangerous glitter in his eyes and the golden smoothness of his skin where the neck met his collar bone. She could not be sure how to interpret his expression. It held both wry amusement, cold assessment, and exasperation. He probably judged her a complete ninny—and she was. Her last vestige of courage had left with Lucy.

"You've come," she said, her voice breathless with fear.

"I'm so glad you've noticed."

"—to . . . *service* me?"

His eyes widened and Allegra cringed as he exploded in a paroxysm of laughter.

"I fail to see the humor," she said stiffly, flames of anger flaring in her chest. He kept chuckling and she longed to shake him into silence. "I expect you to explain," she added with as much starch as she could muster.

He brushed his hand across his eyes and exhaled sharply as his mirth subsided. "Your expression was somewhat unusual," he said, struggling with another bout of mirth. He reached out to pull down the cover, but she tugged it back up and pinched it under her chin.

When he extended his hand again, she flinched back, scooting as far away from him as she could. She feared she would swoon with embarrassment. Not that she had ever swooned in her life, but it might happen, as her life was not yet over. She wished it were. There was a chance she might die with humiliation if he tried to touch her again.

"Skittish, by God," he said with quirk of his lips. "There's no reason to be afraid. Truly, I have no intention of hurting—"

"I don't want—I can't accept . . ." she interrupted, unable to find the words to complete the sentence.

"What? Speak up, wife," he said, his voice harsh. "Do you find me that repulsive?"

"Yes ... *no*," she said, gripping the sheet so hard her hands ached. "I don't know."

"I don't bite, nor do I have a taste for brutalities." He glanced down at her, noticing the paleness of her skin and the dark fear in her eyes. Her alarm annoyed him, and yes, it hurt him that she would care so little for his presence. The rejection smarted. Guilt also nibbled at his heart as he thought about the act he was about to perform. It had nothing to do with love; it was no more than fulfilling a clause in a contract.

"We have to consummate our marriage, make our union complete. It's the law." Exasperated, he watched the sheen of perspiration gather on her forehead. She looked positively green around the mouth. "There's no reason to fear me. Like I said, I'm not a violent man. I shall never lift my hand to you in punishment."

Evidently, judging by her huge frightened eyes, she didn't believe anything he said. "Do you know what such ... intimate union entails, Allegra?"

She shook her head vigorously, and a blush blazed in her cheeks. "No ... but there's no need to take on that hectoring tone of voice with me, milord. I'm not a child."

To be honest, he thought otherwise. He'd been saddled with a little sister who hadn't the faintest notion of how to go on in the world. Except escaping the tyranny of scheming stepfathers.... Very well, he couldn't bed a sister. Her fear had extinguished all desire anyway.

With a sigh, he rose and tucked the down cover closer around her. She flinched and wiggled away. "There, don't fret. I shan't bother you any longer, no more than I would a sister. There will be plenty of time to learn the ways of the world, and I'm not in any particular hurry to ... eh, service you." He suppressed a chuckle and bent over her.

He pressed a light kiss to her damp brow and strode toward his own room. "Good night."

Allegra stared aghast as the door closed behind him. This was not the ending she had envisioned, she knew that much. Yet she should be grateful that she'd won. She wasn't. With his departure, silence and an aching loneliness followed, a feeling of failure. She hadn't pleased him. He'd looked at her indulgently, as if she were a small child who had to be humored. That had hurt more than his uproarious laugh earlier.

She punched the pillow with her fist as inexplicable dissatisfaction washed through her. The condescending mawworm! Giles treated her with more respect, and she *was* his sister.

She stared at the door until her eyes ached. No sounds came from his bedchamber. Evidently he'd gone right to sleep as if nothing out of the ordinary had just happened. Most likely, her presence was a detail that did not need more than his cursory attention.

She turned over and buried her face into the cool linen of the pillowcase. So be it. She could easily match his wintry detachment. She could! Dashing away an annoying tear, she turned her back toward the door that lead to the room of that most odious man.

The next morning Allegra descended the wide red-carpeted stairs in search of breakfast. Lucy had arrived with a cup of cocoa and maintained that it was eight o'clock. Lucy had also informed her that the ladies of London seldom left their bedchambers before noon.

Noon! Not her, Allegra thought, and flung her legs over the side of the bed. Never mind that her head ached, and that her eyelids were weighted down with cannon balls. Lucy had arranged for a bath and chosen a simple blue muslin gown with white dots and a ruffled lace collar for her mistress to wear. Taking a look at herself in the mirror, Allegra thought she had the appearance of a young miss just out of the schoolroom. No wonder Wyndham saw her as a younger sister. *I don't exude a single ounce of sophistication.*

The magnificence of the house with its twenty-foot molded plaster ceilings, towering windows, daunting painted murals of classical motifs, and somber portraits staring down upon her daunted Allegra's spirit. Costly Oriental urns on ebony pedestals, marble tables, and heavy carved pieces in the baroque style of the seventeenth century further reduced her to the country maid who had never seen so many valuable artifacts and gilded moldings gathered under one roof.

She had to ask the lackey standing motionless by the stairs where the breakfast room was located. With a bow, he led the way through a vaulted opening at the other end, and down a corridor to the back of the house. He held a door for her, and she entered a sunny room decorated with a sideboard, a Louis XV commode with chinoiserie panels flanked with torchères, and various china display cabinets.

Dogwood moved in a stately fashion across the carpet and pulled out a Chippendale chair by the round table covered with a white table cloth. The smallness of the table, seating only six, made breakfast an intimate affair. A silver tea service glittered in the bright sunlight.

Allegra gulped when she noticed that the earl had arrived before her. She had hoped to break her fast in peace, but her racing heartbeat told her that peace was not a goal to reach for this morning.

The earl put down the paper by the side of his plate heaped with eggs, ham, and kedgeree. With a decisive nod, he stood and waited until Dogwood had seated her.

"I hope you slept well, my dear," Wyndham said in an impersonal voice.

"Very well, thank you," Allegra said stiffly, while remembering her many hours of tossing and turning. "I pray you had a restful night, milord."

His lips quivered at the corners, and he gave her a glance full of indulgence. "Never slept better."

She could not but notice the vigor of his movements as he attacked the food on his plate. His wavy hair shone and his eyes sparkled. He looked handsome in a bottle-green coat and a pale yellow waistcoat.

Dogwood inquired in morose tones what she wanted to eat.

"Toast and eggs, please, Dogwood," she replied. She stirred her tea agitatedly while waiting for her plate of food to arrive from the nearby sideboard.

Dogwood served her and left, and Allegra almost asked him to remain. The thought of remaining closeted alone with the earl almost overset her. She could barely breathe for the tension building in her chest. Wyndham looked superbly unconcerned as he continued to study the paper at his elbow. She wondered if it was common that gentlemen read the paper on the first morning of their marriage.

"Are you packed for travel, my dear?" he asked blandly.

She nodded. "Yes ... I suppose we're still traveling into Yorkshire."

"Naturally. It is the right thing to do. A wedding without a honeymoon is like a boat without oars."

Allegra could not read the expression in his hooded eyes, but his smile held a world of suggestion. "I think a honeymoon is just what we need."

She blushed and concentrated on her food but found her throat too choked up to swallow much more than tea.

He gave an exasperated sigh. "I believe you received a note with the morning post," the earl said, pointing at a silver salver beside her. Too preoccupied with studying her husband from under lowered lashes, she had not seen the sealed missive.

She opened it eagerly, delighted to discover that Aunt Irene would pay her a morning visit on the following week. She would bring Lydia, a niece from the Sinclair side of the family. Allegra had met Lydia before, in Bath, whence the Sinclairs hailed.

"Irene will call when we return," she said and put down the note.

"It is comforting for you to have a trusted member of the family so close by," Wyndham said without lifting his eyes from the paper. "She might show you around town, introduce you to the fashionable modistes and milliners, and bring you into society."

"You have already furnished me with an excellent wardrobe," Allegra said, unsure how to respond. Her trousseau was even now packed into her traveling cases. She'd spent a whirlwind month of fittings before the wedding, but she'd had no time to explore Bond Street shops or the bazaars.

"I'm certain you need all manner of fripperies and fallals of fashion," he said with a dismissing wave of his hand. "You may have all bills sent to me, and you shall receive your quarterly allowance just as soon as I can draw a bank draft." His eyebrows lifted in sardonic humor. "I hope you shall show some talent for economy and not squander it all in the first month."

"Thank you," she murmured, crushed that he would treat her like an irresponsible child. "I shall endeavor to be a responsible person." Her teacup rattled in the saucer, the only outer show of her inner agitation. He raised his probing blue gaze to her face.

"Is there a problem?" he asked coolly, so calmly in fact that she longed to throw the tea at him.

"No . . . none whatsoever."

He set down his fork, seemingly in control of himself and the world. "Good. I'm glad you're settling in."

Allegra suppressed an urge to cry. Feeling more like a guest than the mistress of the house, she glanced at her intimidating "host." She wondered if he sensed her discomfort, and cursed herself for her lack of polish. If only she weren't so inexperienced in the ways of society! After meeting some of the earl's cronies and their wives at the wedding, Allegra feared that she would never acquire such town polish as they possessed.

She watched as her husband stirred the mound of scrambled eggs in irritation.

"Are the eggs not fresh?" she ventured to ask after dabbing at her mouth with her napkin.

"Eggs!" he said. "I swear Leon, the cook, is deaf. I don't know how many times I've asked for a boiled egg, but he forgets and serves this gluey mash. Cold it is to boot."

"I recall that Mr. Harcombe—Percy—complimented your chef."

"Yes," he replied with a laugh. "But Percy does not eat eggs." He put down his napkin decisively and glared at Allegra. She flinched, but tried to put a smile on her lips.

"My dear," he said, "what are your plans for after our trip? Will you stay in London for the rest of the season, or do you desire to go down to High Wyndham?"

Allegra tried to gather her wits, wondering what would be the right answer. She wished she could muster some of her usual buoyancy, but not only did the earl daunt her after last night's failure, but his magnificent home did as well. "I have no plans except to receive my aunt when we return."

"Very well," he said in a clipped voice. "When we return you shall be presented to the Queen. Before we go, I shall introduce you to the staff. You've already met Dogwood, and Lucy, the kitchen maid. There's the housekeeper, Mrs. Buxton, and the various maids and footmen. You might as well familiarize yourself with the running of the household."

"That is desirable," she said, but wishing she were a thousand miles away.

"You shall in due course hire an abigail for your personal use. I'm certain that Lucy will not do in the long run."

"Lucy ... appears to be a friendly sort of person," Allegra said, remembering her first startling meeting with the outspoken maid. "Knowledgeable of all details—"

"But not in possession of the polish expected in a lady's maid." The earl's lips slanted with amusement. "I suppose Lucy is hardworking and cheerful, but not what you would like to see doing—"

"She's loyal and capable," Allegra interrupted, nettled. It galled her that the earl had the nerve to tell her how to judge the servants. "In fact, if she so desires, Lucy shall be promoted to lady's maid."

His eyes narrowed with distaste. "Is that a wise choice?"

Allegra tried to quell the trepidation that came in the wake of her rebellion. His attitude made her hackles rise, but she had acted rashly. Yet ... "As you've pointed out, I am now the mistress of the house."

He flung down his napkin with a grim smile. "So you are. Well, as soon as I've introduced you to the staff, I'll leave you to get ready for the trip."

The tension swelled in the room until Allegra could not choke down another morsel of food. She pushed aside the plate as she sensed his impatience. He summoned Dogwood and asked that the servants be assembled in the hallway.

Allegra gulped down some tea, waiting uneasily while the earl stood by the window, his back turned toward her.

Dogwood returned ten minutes later, just at the moment when Allegra thought she would break down and cry. She felt Wyndham's impatience like a sour cloak upon her. Unable to raise her eyes to his face, she followed him into the hallway.

The checkered marble floor of the foyer swayed and tilted before her eyes as if taking on a life of its own. Her stomach had folded itself into a wad, and fear had made her hands clammy. The servants formed two lines, one female, one male. Blurry faces, starched caps and aprons, silver-and-black livery, and a welter of names danced before Allegra's eyes and ears, but she managed to find a smile for everyone. What a stern-faced lot, she thought, as she noticed the servants' haughty expressions. Seemingly, they took more pride in their lofty station than the earl did in his. Their eyes let her know that she would have to earn their respect.

"When we get back, Mrs. Buxton will show you all the rooms and the storage areas," the earl said in bored tones.

Allegra nodded, her gaze landing upon Lucy, who was next to last in the row, beside the scullery maid. Lucy winked and smiled, unthinkable behavior in a servant, but the impudent act warmed Allegra's heart.

Dogwood cleared his throat pompously. "On behalf of the servants, I'd like to wish you welcome, Lady Wyndham. We look forward to waiting upon you."

Allegra took a deep breath. "Thank you all." She felt the hot flush of mortification stain her cheeks, and she cursed herself. Hooking on to Lucy's encouraging smile, she managed a smile in response.

"I'm sure we'll get along famously," she said in as firm a voice as she could muster. The earl gave her an approving nod and left the hallway. His departure left her floundering, as if in a deep sea, and she'd better start swimming, or she would never inspire respect in the servants.

chapter 6

If Bonaparte considered the battle of Waterloo a complete disaster, Allegra judged that Boney's defeat had been small in comparison with the tragedy of her honeymoon.

If Wyndham had hoped that she would come about, become the self-assured and accomplished countess that would make him a happy bridegroom and bring pride to his name, he was sorely mistaken. Not only had her conversations lacked any degree of finesse, her bedtime procedure had become a hasty retreat under quilts and blankets that were sure to keep him at bay. He hadn't even once tried to scale the bastion of her high-necked nightgowns with their armor of tiny buttons.

He had taken one look at her on the first night in their joint bedchamber and retreated to a lumpy cot in the dressing room. "I will not force myself upon your person," he'd said. From then on, his anger and exasperation turned into icy politeness, and Allegra's defense became a wall of silence.

Upon returning to London, he voiced that he would shortly travel into Somerset to see to his estates. Allegra wasted no time fleeing to her chambers with the excuse of overseeing the unpacking of her things.

That night she heard from Lucy, who'd heard it from

Oglesby, Wyndham's valet, that the earl had taken refuge in his old pastimes: He'd dined at the club and later attended a mill on the outskirts of London.

The next day Allegra took stock of all the linen closets and storerooms of the great mansion. Dogwood took her on a tour of the wine cellars, his sole domain, and the stillroom. The unsmiling Mrs. Buxton took pride in showing her the gleaming and spotless guest rooms, all ten of them, and the ballroom with its gilt moldings, mirrors, and sculpted plaster ceiling. The drawing and morning rooms, and the various salons off the hallway. The only area that she didn't examine was the library. The earl brooded there in deep silence and had left orders that he was not to be disturbed.

Aunt Irene and Lydia Sinclair arrived when Allegra thought she could not bear another second in the house.

"There you are, darling niece," Aunt Irene greeted. She gave her young relative a hug, and Allegra rested her tired brow upon her aunt's shoulder. "You look worn to a shade."

"I never realized how much there is to remember about the management of a grand household like this. It's nothing like home, where I used to supervise the maids quite well. I don't see how I'll ever prevail. My head is spinning like a top."

Allegra felt Aunt Irene's searching gaze upon her, and she was sure her aunt could read the misery in her face. Still, shame lay too heavily on Allegra's mind for any confidences. She had no desire to divulge the failure of her honeymoon to kind Aunt Irene. She pushed her heavy misgivings to the side and forced a bright smile to her lips.

Lydia, a sprite of a woman with birdlike features and a long slender neck, danced up the stairs ahead of them. She wore a pomona green silk spencer with fitted sleeves puffed at the top, a flounced gown of French cambric, and a dashing hat adorned with a curling ostrich feather and a wide green ribbon tied under her pert chin. She could have stepped out of a fashion plate from *La Belle Assemblée*. Allegra wondered if she would ever acquire such dash and style.

Lydia's brown eyes sparkled with interest as Allegra ushered them into her private parlor. Her gaze traveled from the Oriental-style chaise longue with its gilt dragon feet, to Chippendale armchairs, and the mother-of-pearl inlaid escritoire. A sea of lozenge-and-flower patterned carpet did nothing to make the room more cozy, Allegra thought.

"This is grand, fit for a duchess!" Lydia exclaimed and clapped her hands together in delight. "I declare you're the luckiest female alive," she added and gave Allegra a warm hug.

Allegra smiled wryly, forgetting the trying morning of parrying Mrs. Buxton's thrusts to preserve her power in the household. "I've always been graced with uncommon luck." She touched the old gold locket pinned to her bodice. "My four-leaf clover is proof of that, but I fear that I shall *disappear* in this vast chamber and never find my way out."

Lydia's laugh tinkled. "Nonsense! You will soon learn to be a grand lady, just as befits your station." She pulled Allegra with her to an arrangement of sofa and chairs by the fireplace. An embroidered firescreen graced the empty grate, and fresh flowers adorned the table.

They sat down, Allegra in the middle, and her two guests on each side of her. Lydia chattered about the latest gossip as she took off her hat. Her hair bounced in fashionable ringlets around her ears, and Allegra decided she would have her hair done in this latest style.

"Let me introduce my friend"—Lydia contorted her voice to a pompous drawl—"the Countess of Wyndham.

Wife of the most esteemed and elevated seventh Earl of Wyndham."

"Oh, have done!" Allegra admonished and elbowed her friend in the side. "After spending a year in London, you Lydia, would fit the role with great aplomb."

"The London modistes can gild any old copper pot, Allegra. Now you must tell us about your honeymoon. I want to know every sordid detail."

Allegra cursed the blush rising in her cheeks and looked away. "Nothing much to tell, really. We rode in the morning and explored the old mansion in the afternoon."

"And the evenings?" Lydia asked breathlessly. "What did you do?"

Allegra sought for a light answer but could find none. Too mortified to speak of her failures, she mentioned the weather. "It rained most evenings."

Aunt Irene hadn't said much, only glancing now and again at Allegra's face. "Are you happy?" she asked at last.

"Yes," Lydia chimed in, "do you adore your new life and your handsome husband? He was a prize catch until you came along and stole him."

Allegra experienced a surge of sadness, which she desperately tried to tuck into the farthest corner of her mind. "Of course I'm happy," she said, hearing the false note in her voice. "Why shouldn't I be? I've caught the most eligible gentleman in town—from right under the noses of desperate matchmaking mamas, and I've just spent a week with him in romantic solitude."

Lydia said, "That you did, and tweaked Justine's nose in the bargain. It was addle-brained of her to jilt the earl, but love moves in mysterious ways. The foolish girl has her heart set on Lord Lewington, the worst rake in history."

Allegra gasped for air as if her stays had been pulled too tightly. "I have not yet seen Justine, since coming to

London, but I'm bound to run into her at some gathering. I suspect 'twill be an unpleasant encounter. Invitations to every function are already flowing in."

"You shall come through the ordeal well enough. Justine is not one to bear a grudge. I'm not sure how well the earl will hold up," Lydia said thoughtlessly, then slapped her hand to her mouth. "Don't take any heed to me, Allegra. My tongue is as usual running away with me."

"What difficulties the earl experiences in Justine's presence is none of my business," Allegra said stiffly. "If he's still carrying the torch for her, there's nothing I can do to change his feelings."

Lydia's eyes widened. "But there is! With some modicum of finesse you're bound to wind him around your little finger." She laughed and wiggled her tiny slippered foot. "When has a gentleman ever been a match for a woman's wiles?"

Allegra gaped in shock. "I have no intention of *luring* the earl with female wiles." She stood, emotions storming her defenses, her legs trembling most abominably.

Aunt Irene nodded her approval. "That is commendable, dear Allegra. In due time he will recognize your many fine qualities and congratulate himself for his great choice of wife. Gentlemen will not hesitate to take the credit for their mate's accomplishments." She nodded sagely. "I know that from my marriage to Sinclair. If you become a brilliant hostess, Wyndham will bask in the compliments you reap."

"I shall ring for refreshments." To get away from their searching stares, Allegra crossed the room and tugged the bellpull. She had no difficulty picturing herself a good hostess. Mama had never had any interest in the Temple household affairs, and the responsibility to make the house run smoothly had fallen on Allegra's shoulders the year Pinkney took her out of the ladies' academy.

One of the footmen entered to take her order of iced cakes and ratafia to Dogwood downstairs.

"You'll have to impress the earl with a display of wifely competence," Lydia said. "Make sure he's only served his favorite dishes. See to it that his port bottle is never empty."

"Mrs. Buxton is a competent housekeeper, and surely Dogwood fills all decanters daily." Allegra could not think of many favors that would impress her husband. As a married couple, they were eons apart, she the moon, he the sun. She had no inkling how to span the gap, how to make a bridge of stars across the void. Shocked, she realized that she wanted nothing as much as to touch his heart.

The realization made Allegra speechless. When had she started to care about the earl's preferences and opinions, about his heart? Perhaps when he'd revealed that behind the intimidating facade was a gentleman who'd known little love and parental affection in his life.

"Justine is impatient to see you," Lydia said. "For obvious reasons she couldn't very well attend the wedding."

"Despite what has happened, I still count her as my friend," Allegra said. She lifted up the kitten who had come to investigate the party. His coat shone black and silky. His purr warmed her as she scratched one pointed ear.

After Dogwood had delivered a tray of refreshments, and the cakes had been sampled, Aunt Irene suggested, "Would you like to accompany us to Bond Street, my dear? Lydia has fittings for a ball gown, and I'm going to purchase a birthday gift."

Allegra nodded, glad to get out of the oppressive house and away from the husband who brought out all her insecurities. She set down the kitten. "I shall like that above all things. Let me fetch my pelisse and bonnet."

As they stepped downstairs, they encountered the earl in the hallway. He was pulling on his gloves, his walking cane clamped under one arm. Reluctant to meet him, Allegra halted on the stairs behind the others.

"Ladies," he greeted with a charming smile. He gave Allegra a questioning glance. "Are you going out?"

"Yes," she said, convulsively clutching her reticule against her middle. Why did her legs turn into blancmange every time she encountered Wyndham? Surely he'd done nothing to warrant such inner turmoil.

"May I request a seat in your carriage, Mrs. Sinclair? I had planned to walk to my club, but this would give me an opportunity for company," he said smoothly. "I'm in a talkative mood."

Aunt Irene smiled graciously. "Of course you may go with us, Ian. Need you ask? We'll let you off on Bond Street."

Allegra viewed his broad back as he offered her aunt his arm. *Ian.* Just imagine that Aunt Irene, who had only known the earl scant weeks, ventured to call him by his first name. Allegra wished she dared to show such spirit, but after a week of humiliation, all her courage seemed to have abandoned her.

They went out to the waiting carriage. Allegra trembled as his hand closed around hers, the warmth of him penetrating her glove. She was eager, yet loath to relinquish his hold as he aided her up the step and into the Sinclair barouche. He gave her a hooded glance, a glance that set her heart fluttering. Why did such opposite emotions fly through her in his presence?

The spring morning shone like a bright new gold coin. Not a cloud marred the azure sky. The din of London did not penetrate this far into Mayfair, but the closer the carriage came to the merchant streets, the echoes of shouts, the lash of whips, and the creak of unoiled wheels increased.

"I suppose you ladies have nothing better to do than to squander your funds on fallals of fashion," the earl said with a teasing grin.

Allegra's volatile temper rose in defense, and before intimidation took over, she burst out, "That's monstrously unfair, my lord. Gentlemen squander their fortunes on such useless pastimes as gambling and betting."

He gave her an amused glance. "You're right on that score, Allegra. Highly irresponsible of us. I daresay we're a great group of muttonheads."

Allegra blushed, aghast that she'd blurted out a criticism when he'd only been funning. She lowered her eyes, mauling the tassel of her brocade reticule between her fingers.

"At least we have items to show from our forages into the shops," Lydia said practically. "Sometimes things of great value."

"Yes . . . I suppose a ball gown is not a trifle to be had for sixpence."

Allegra lifted her gaze to her husband's face, seeing the humorous sparkle in his eyes. She had not realized how attractive a laugh he had, but then, he'd had little reason to laugh in her company. The sun picked out a dent on the left side of his lips when he smiled. She had an overwhelming urge to trace her finger over that indentation, and along the hard jawline. Mortified at the wanton desires racing in her blood, she stared at everything except the earl.

The barouche arrived at the corner of Bruton Street, and the cacophony of noise rose to an angry pitch as the horses turned onto Bond Street.

"Well, look at that!" said Aunt Irene. "A coaching accident. Our passage will be delayed for an hour at least.

Mayhap we should ask the driver to turn around. That is, if he can do it in this melee."

Allegra studied with interest two coachmen who had embroiled their limbs in a kicking and boxing match. Two horses milled shackleless along the street, and a flower seller screamed her abuse as she returned crushed bouquets to her overturned basket.

"Yes, the axle is broken on one vehicle, and the other is so large, it'll take ten men to set it back on its wheels," Wyndham said thoughtfully.

Allegra watched as someone rolled a wheel along the cobbles. She stared in surprise as a hand, belonging to a grimy urchin, flashed into a gentleman's pocket. The robbed onlooker whirled around and let out a shout. Shaking her head in wonder, she watched as the gentleman sprinted in pursuit of the robber. To her amazement, he gripped the arm of another filthy street boy, thinking he'd apprehended the thief who was now hiding under a wagon. The man lifted his whip and began applying its hissing thong to the boy's back.

"Look! He's whipping the wrong person. The thief is over there." Allegra pointed toward the wagon, but the urchin had disappeared in the throng.

The innocent boy squealed in pain every time the whip lashed his back. Allegra rose as if feeling the sting on her own back. "I have to do something! The man's hurting an innocent child." She began fumbling with the door latch, but Wyndham put a restraining hand on her arm.

"Don't take on so, Allegra. Theft and punishment is a common sight in London."

"He's innocent," she went on, tears rising to her eyes. "It's too shocking by half. You'll have to help him."

She gave her husband a pleading stare, and he returned it broodingly. "Sit down, Allegra. Don't worry yourself. I'll take care of it." His jaw set into a decisive line, he jumped down and pushed his way across the congested street. Allegra followed his progress breathlessly.

With a quick movement the earl twisted the whip from the stranger's hand. His face set in hard lines, he beckoned and spoke. She wished she could hear the conversation over the din, but she could only watch as the stranger gesticulated wildly and shouted in anger. Allegra thought he would attack Wyndham, but the earl spoke sharply and hauled the urchin to his feet. He turned the ruffian's pockets inside out, finding them empty.

The stranger threw his arms in the air, his florid face a study of exasperation. Wyndham handed over the whip with a shrug of his shoulders, and the stranger stomped off.

The urchin, grimy hat in hand, said something as he looked up into the earl's face. The earl smiled grimly and pointed straight at Allegra. She swallowed hard, wondering if the earl was angry with her.

To her surprise, the urchin loped across the street and halted below the carriage. "Thankee, ma'am, for savin' me life," the boy said, and smiled, his teeth surprisingly white in the dirty face. "I'm ever so grateful." He was older than she'd previously deduced by his small size, about ten years, she guessed.

"I'll say!" Aunt Irene expostulated and fanned herself.

Wyndham arrived to stand over the youngster. "You're fortunate that Lady Wyndham saw your plight, but mayhap you were waiting for the right moment to relieve some other gentleman of his snuffbox."

"How can you be so cruel as to accuse him of planning thievery!" Allegra admonished. "The boy is a beggar, naught but skin and bones."

"Aye, melady, I be a poor wee beggar," the urchin said with a twinkle in his eye. He hauled a wooden bowl from the inside of his filthy shirt. "A groat for a starvin' child, if ye pleeeease."

Wyndham snorted and jumped into the barouche, slamming the door behind him. "Take your theatricals elsewhere, Tom."

"Tom's not me name, melord. I'm Knocky Martin, proud owner of a pair of fives that would knock th' living daylights out o' the finest pugilist at Cribb's Parlor."

Wyndham laughed derisively. "And a ready tongue in your head."

Allegra glanced down into the merry eyes of the beggar, a plan forming in her head. "Are you quick on your legs, Knocky?"

"Course I am, melady." He wiped his nose with the back of his hand. "Me pins are the fastest of any beggar from Whitechapel to Spitalfields."

"Well, you're far away from home, Knocky," Wyndham said with dry sarcasm. "Ready to relieve the Mayfair inhabitants of their purses, no doubt."

"He said he's a beggar." Allegra gave the earl a dark look, and Aunt Irene and Lydia exchanged amused smiles.

"That's God's truth," Knocky said, shaking his cracked bowl.

Allegra took a deep breath. She refused to look at Wyndham as she leaned forward to speak with the youth. "Why is it that you don't have honest work, Knocky? After all, you've told us you're in the prime of health."

Knocky's face took on an air of outrage. "Work, melady? There's none to be 'ad, and who would 'ire a beggar? I 'ave ten brothers and sisters, none o' them workin'. Me father, God rest 'is soul, drowned in th' London docks. Too much blue ruin under 'is belt."

Blue ruin? Allegra's head spun with all the information. She liked the boy's merry glint and ready smile.

"Let's be on our way," Wyndham said as he craned his

neck to view the accident site. "Looks as if we might make a turn."

"Wait!" Allegra cried as he ordered the coachman to turn the vehicle. The carriage jolted to a halt. "Would you like to have decent work, Knocky? Make your honest living as my page? Run errands for me? Generally be at my beck and call in a great house?"

"I would thank me Maker ever' day o' me life!"

"This is lunacy," Wyndham muttered under his breath, but he did not protest as Allegra opened the door and beckoned the boy inside. Aunt Irene looked askance at the boy's grimy legs and feet folding themselves readily upon the floor of the carriage.

"Ye are a livin' breathin' angel, melady," Knocky said with a huge smile at Allegra. "One o' God's white angels."

"Does he have fleas?" Lydia asked *sotto voce* and moved the hem of her gown as far as she could from the tattered and foul-smelling urchin.

Allegra viewed the boy's blond thatch of hair with misgiving. "I surely hope not." She sent her husband an uneasy glance, fully expecting his face to be wrathful. Rubbing his chin in thought, however, he looked rather dazed than angry. She feared he would give her a rakedown at home.

That fear tied itself into a hard knot in her stomach as the barouche rumbled back to Berkley Square to deliver Knocky into Dogwood's horrified arms.

Wyndham did not say another word during the return trip to Bond Street via Hay Hill and Grafton Street. The carriage halted at the milliner shop, and the earl got out to assist the ladies down. Allegra's hand trembled in his, and his forceful grip made her look up into his face. She saw only cool indifference and hastily averted her gaze.

"La! What an eventful morning!" Lydia cried as she

joined Allegra in front of the milliner's. "I daresay you have the softest heart of anyone I know, Allegra, and quite an adventurous spirit."

"That is a misstatement," the earl muttered. As he helped Aunt Irene down, the door to the shop opened and two ladies stepped outside. One of them a lady's maid, the other a young lady dressed in a striped silk pelisse and matching bonnet.

Allegra gasped as she looked into Justine Bryerly's wide blue eyes. Justine's face, as lovely as a rose, and eyes as brilliant as diamonds, made Allegra's knees weak with worry.

"Justine!" Lydia called out. "How fortunate. I was going to call on you this morning."

Justine's gaze flickered from Allegra's face to the earl, standing right behind her. The street seemed to turn into a swaying bog, and Allegra thought she would swoon with humiliation.

Justine lifted her chin in the air and straightened her back. Two red spots glowed high in her cheeks. "Allegra ... Lord Wyndham, I ... wanted you to know that I wish you the very best." She gave the earl a measuring glance. "I never knew you were capable of such a rash action as a hasty marriage," she added. "I'm pleasantly surprised."

"Impulsive acts sometimes enliven one's life. I hate to think that the *ton* labeled me a complete bore, after you did," he replied, a world of disdain in his voice.

Allegra looked at him, the pointed fangs of jealousy biting into her heart. His face had paled and held a stricken expression, his eyes dark, his lips set into a grim line. However hard he tried, he couldn't hide his emotions. *He still loves Justine,* Allegra thought with a sinking feeling. And who wouldn't, seeing her rosy complexion, sparkling eyes, and classical features? Justine was not the reigning toast of the *ton* for nothing.

"I suppose there are hidden sides to every person until certain situations come along to reveal them," Justine replied with an edge to her voice. "Or someone manages to open the hardened heart."

Silence lingered, but the tension dispersed as Justine turned away from the earl and smiled at Allegra. "Imagine that! You beat me to the altar. Who would have thought that Mr. Pinkney would let you out of Chippenham to the fleshpots of London?"

Allegra forced a smile to her lips and gave the earl a sideways glance. He looked surprised, evidently unaware of her friendship with Justine. He moved away to respond to an inquiry by the coachman. "Fate plays in mysterious ways."

"Very mysterious, and—unexpected." Justine smiled. "It must have been the influence of your lucky clover."

"Of course." Allegra laughed, grateful that Justine was trying to lighten the mood. "To tell you the truth, Pinkney was not pleased to let me go but had to yield to a more determined mind." Saying those words, Allegra realized that she was very pleased with her change in fortune, despite the intimidation she felt in the earl's presence.

"Any fate would be better than living under Mr. Pinkney's rule." Justine gave a last speaking glance at the earl, who stood silently watching her from afar.

"Yes," Allegra replied. "I'm starting a new life." She placed her hand on Justine's arm, wondering if she still had the friend she'd made during her time at the young ladies' academy in Bath. "I hope you'll be part of it. Come for a visit soon."

Justine flashed a smile. "Thank you." She pressed Allegra's hand. " 'Til later, then." She left with her maid, waving at the others.

Allegra turned to her husband. "I pray you don't mind that I invited Justine."

He smiled noncommittally, the stark pain still evident in his eyes. "What you do with your days is your business, not mine," he said.

Allegra's knees melted as he placed a perfunctory kiss on her cheek, bowed to the other ladies, and strode in the direction of his club. As he left, Allegra noticed that some of the bright light had gone out of her day.

Dazed, Wyndham sauntered toward White's, his thoughts crashing around the memory of Justine's bright eyes. He'd quite forgotten how lovely she was, and how sparkling a character lay beyond all that beauty. *Oh, God,* he wanted to moan out loud, disgusted with himself for his weak heart. He was married, dammit all. He couldn't very well hanker after a female he couldn't have, but there was no ordering his wayward heart to complying with his wishes.

Rotten worm, he castigated himself. Heaving a deep sigh, he remembered the complete failure of the honeymoon in Yorkshire. He compressed his jaws so hard he thought they would crack. If only Allegra saw it in her heart to let him into her bed, he might have a chance to forget Justine Bryerly—in time.

He would have to work hard at it, find a way to overcome the overwhelming memories of his erstwhile fiancée. Overcome his weakness. Filled with misgivings, he wasn't sure he was up to the challenge, and that would be monstrously unfair to his young bride.

chapter 7

The next morning Allegra came downstairs after spending an uncomfortable night mulling over Wyndham and his love for Justine Bryerly. A lowering subject, which made her feel young and inexperienced. She'd heard, by the sounds coming from the adjoining bedchamber, that her husband had returned home late. His boots had thudded against the floor, and he'd talked with his valet, Oglesby, in subdued tones.

What had been so important that he preferred to stay away from home rather than share dinner with her? She knew the answer, and it depressed her. *Any* pastime held more allure than her company. After seeing Justine, he probably loathed the thought of going home and being reminded of his less than perfect marriage.

No wonder she couldn't sleep.

She made her way across the hallway, by now slightly less in awe of the painted deities on the walls and the hollow stillness of the lofty rooms. Mrs. Buxton was beginning to thaw, and Knocky greeted her in the corridor leading to the breakfast parlor, strutting around in his black-and-silver livery. Cleaned of all grime, he was an attractive boy.

"How do you like it here, Knocky?" she asked.

"Cor, a real cot to sleep in, a blanket that's more wool than 'oles, and food *three* times a day. 'Tis better than life at Carlton House, melady." He grasped her hand as if to kiss it, and Dogwood, who'd just entered, cleared his throat forcefully.

Knocky shrugged and dropped her hand. "I'm ever so grateful. The noddys wot's workin' fer ya is a starched set of dullswifts, but despite 'em chips, this is wot yer call paradise."

Dogwood's brow grew dark, and Knocky swaggered toward the door that led down to the kitchens. "I'll go down an' lend a 'elpin' 'and to that barmy Frenchman. Doesn't know 'is 'ead from a 'ole in the ground."

Flashing a grin, Knocky disappeared, and Allegra shook her head in bemusement. "I daresay he'll learn the ways of the house in a trice," she said to Dogwood's forbidding countenance.

"I *daresay*," Dogwood said at his very driest.

Stifling a smile, she hurried into the breakfast parlor. She hoped, as the day was still young, that Wyndham had not ventured out of his room. But to her chagrin, she found him at the table. She gulped down a wave of tension and forced a bright smile to her face. "Good morning, milord," she said.

Wyndham lifted his gaze from the newspaper. "A good morning it is not in my opinion."

Allegra slid into her seat, her elbow knocking over an empty teacup. She righted it with unsteady hands.

The butler looked more lugubrious than ever as he stepped up to the sideboard. He bore an expression much like the weather, a curtain of gray skies and a steady trickle of rain. It pattered softly against the windows.

"I pray you spent a peaceful night," the earl said with a sardonic lift of eyebrows.

Allegra feared that he could see right through her. She

averted her gaze and swallowed convulsively. "Very well, thank you," she lied.

Dogwood brought a cup of steaming coffee, and Allegra sipped gratefully, hoping to disperse the gluey fog of sleeplessness in her mind. "And you, milord?" she asked, staring at Dogwood's back as he left the room.

"Likewise," he said indifferently and buried his face behind the morning paper.

"Milord . . ." she began, "I never informed you of my friendship with Justine Bryerly. Does it bother you?"

"No, why should it?" He held the paper like a shield. "I'd rather not talk about her."

The room filled with an uncomfortable silence. Dogwood returned. "Hrrumph." He cleared his throat pointedly, and Allegra looked at him.

"Sorry to disturb your breakfast, milord, but I find this new fellow, Lady Wyndham's page, highly uncouth, and if I may say so, very *unnerving*."

"Knocky? What's wrong with the boy?" Wyndham asked, with a flash of amusement in his eyes. "Has he taken off with the silver already?"

Dogwood looked aghast and sniffed. "*Not at all*, milord, I keep *that* under lock and key at all times. No"—he threw an apologetic glance at Allegra—"he sings, milord. I might add that he does not cast me in mind of the Opera artists—rather something more vulgar. A rare lot of caterwauling, milord!"

"He sings at his tasks? What exact chores have you allotted to him when he's not running errands?"

"Well . . . after his three, much-needed baths, I set him to work helping the maids shifting heavy furniture in the music parlor. Lady Wyndham asked to have it cleaned."

"Excellent!" Wyndham gave Allegra an appreciative smile that set her heart racing.

"Well, it's just that he not only sings, he plays the

pianoforte as well. I had to bodily remove him from the music room—with the help of two footmen." Dogwood emitted a series of sniffs to underscore his deeply disturbed sense of propriety.

The earl rubbed his chin in thought. "Seems that the fellow has many talents."

"*Too* many, if you ask me, milord." Dogwood raised his nose in the air. "Knocky is a disrespectful young jackanapes."

The earl winked at Allegra from the edge of the newspaper, and her heart made a ridiculous jolt of pleasure. Evidently his meeting with Justine had not completely thrown him into the pits of gloom.

Wyndham continued: "Dogwood, are you implying that Knocky has no business working here?"

Dogwood cleared his throat anew. "This is at the very center of my thoughts, milord."

"I think Her Ladyship would be very disappointed if we were to kick the boy back onto the street. She's bent on reforming his young life, you see. Rather make a silk purse out of a sow's ear."

"If I may be so bold, that will not be possible." Dogwood gave his mistress a disapproving stare but hastily diverted it as Allegra returned a firm one of her own. Silence hovered uncomfortably in the room.

"Her Ladyship might prove you wrong. I vote the boy will stay for now," the earl said, dismissing the butler.

"I daresay the *creature* will improve with time," Dogwood said with a sniff. His back looked stiffly offended as he left the room.

"Thank you, milord, for supporting me," Allegra said as the door closed. "Dogwood can be so very intimidating."

Wyndham hid his smile behind the napkin, but Allegra sensed his approval and was ridiculously pleased. She spread jam on a piece of toast. She bit into the crispy bread and noticed Wyndham's thoughtful gaze upon her face. A warm blush crept into her face.

He pointed at his plate. "I take it you're behind this new regimen of boiled eggs? I'm delighted. Tell me, how did you change Leon's inflexible mind?"

Allegra puffed up with delight at his praise. "I simply told him I would hire another chef lest he change his ways. Lucy informed me that he shoved some copper pots to the floor in a fit of temper after I left. She also pointed out that I was the first countess she'd ever known to enter the nether regions of the house."

"She's probably right, but I doubt that she's met more than one countess in her life," he said dryly. "She's very fortunate to have her star rise in such meteoric fashion—thanks to you."

"Lucy is proficient at many things, most of all talking, and—gossiping. She has also made a friend of Knocky."

"You're full of surprises, Allegra. What's next besides surrounding yourself, and me, with unconventional servants? A pet tiger? Mayhap this gloomy mansion needs the music of a dexterous pickpocket and the ministrations of a Drury Lane gabblemonger to come alive."

"Lucy is not a gabblemonger," Allegra said firmly. "Only extremely talkative."

"I shall eat my egg and be quiet," the earl drawled. He set to the task while Allegra opened a stack of mail by her plate.

"We've been invited to the Duchess of Newberry's ball in four weeks," she said. "Are we to attend?"

"You'll have to be presented at the Queen's Drawing Room before you can attend any functions. Percy's mother, Mrs. Harcombe, has agreed to introduce you next week."

"Aunt Irene has arranged for a Court dress." Allegra cringed at the thought of standing eye to eye with the

Queen and the Prince Regent. "I'm not sure I'm ready to meet the Queen, but a ball is another matter altogether."

"You shall contrive splendidly, my dear. The Queen might be high in the instep, but she's a kind lady. I suppose I could escort you to Newberry House. Mind you, the ball will be a dead bore. Expect no more than watered sherry and stale cakes for midnight refreshments. Newberry is notoriously tight-fisted."

"We could possibly bring a picnic hamper."

The earl smiled sardonically. "And spread out a tablecloth in the middle of the dance floor. We might as well bring food for all the guests. Everyone will be hungry."

Allegra almost choked on her tea at the thought of guests sitting in a ring on the floor, eating lobster patties and syllabubs.

"And we shall bring Knocky along for entertainment." She leaned forward, touching his arm in excitement. "In fact, we could invite people here for a humorous musical evening. I don't think such an event has occurred before in London."

He glanced at her hand still on his sleeve, and, immediately self-conscious, she pulled away. "The matrons will be shocked," he said, "but I like the idea. We would, however, become the laughingstock of polite society."

The earl had a point. A deadly boring musicale was *de rigueur*, not some spectacle inspired by the bawdy theaters. Still, the possibilities enticed her.

He patted her hand in a brotherly fashion. "You have a lively imagination, Allegra."

"Ditto."

They stared at each other for a long moment, and Allegra almost choked on the emotion rising in her chest. She wished she could see love and admiration, not just brotherly approval in his silver-blue eyes.

The realization jolted her senses. She had to admit to

herself that she'd fallen head over heels into love with her husband. The knowledge dazed and frightened her—rankled, too. What if he never found it in his heart to return her love? She would live the rest of her days in misery.

He got up and patted her shoulder. "It has stopped raining. Would you like to take a ride in the park before the next shower attacks?"

Delighted that he cared enough to ask, she nodded and put aside the stack of invitations. She might as well savor the unexpectedly peaceful feeling between them, make the most of his favors while she still had them.

Green Park sat like an emerald jewel in veils of mist. Crystal raindrops glinted on every leaf and hung in garlands on the spiderwebs spanning the branches. Cottony gray clouds sailed low across the sky, bearing the promise of more rain. The sandy lanes and paths had been abandoned by the usual morning riders, leaving silent and damp desolation behind.

The earl rode Thunder, a frisky gray stallion, and Allegra was mounted on a more docile mare, a chestnut with black stockings named Sable. The mare did have a sable soft coat, Allegra thought as she patted the silky neck. The horse slowed to a walk after a brisk trot.

The long blue veil of her hat fluttered behind her, and she struggled to wind it back around the crown.

She threw a glance at the earl, who looked exceptionally handsome in an immaculately cut riding coat of dark blue wool, a perfect neckcloth, and a beaver at a rakish angle on his head. His attractive appearance affected her heart until it ached, and she longed to express her feelings.

He pulled up next to her and halted both mounts by gripping her reins. He was so close his knee rubbed against hers, and he leaned across and rewrapped the unruly veil around her high-crowned hat. She waited in breathless silence as she watched his solemn face so close she could easily have touched him.

The wind rattled raindrops out of the ancient oak, spattering everything. She laughed as a drop touched her nose. He glanced at her in surprise, then shared her merriment.

His warm hand rested on her shoulder, then cupped her neck, pulling her slowly forward until her face was so close she could feel his warm breath wafting over her. She could neither breathe nor think as his lips touched hers so lightly it could have been the wings of a butterfly fluttering against her lips. She shivered in pleasure, waiting, hoping for more, but he only looked deeply into her eyes, and she struggled to read the expression in his. She saw affection, certainly, and surprise, and questions—many questions.

She gasped and pulled away, unable to stand the suspense of waiting for his renewed attention. The touch of his mouth still burned on her lips as if applied with inexplicable heat.

"We ... we'd better go on," she whispered at last. "It'll rain by the look of those dark clouds." She pointed ahead, and as she evaluated the approaching rain, she noticed a rider coming from the other direction of the soggy path.

Wyndham seemed reluctant to relinquish his hold on her. He sighed and dropped his hand away from her arm.

"Look, another rider who dared to challenge the elements," she said breathlessly.

"By Jove, it's Perce," the earl said. "I'm surprised. He does not like rain on his cravat."

Percy shouted a greeting and pulled up his horse beside them. "Good morning, fairest one," he said with his kind twinkle and bent over Allegra's hand.

Wyndham snorted. "You could have knocked me over with a feather when I saw you on the path, Perce. Something momentous must have happened to bring you out in the rain."

"A little rain does not dissolve a man," Percy scoffed. "My person—if you excuse my vulgarity—is watertight."

"I could take an oath that you hate to get rain upon your starched shirtpoints," the earl said with a laugh. "They are positively wilting now."

Percy's already florid complexion turned crimson. "If you must know," he said in an undertone, "I am of a mind to reduce my circumference. Dashed difficult under the current situation to find some nubile maiden who'll form a *tendre* for this rotund individual." He threw a shy glance at Allegra, who was hard put not to laugh. She composed herself and turned a serious face toward him.

"Any female would be flattered to earn your attention," she said gravely.

He fluttered a hand impatiently. "You're most kind, Allegra. For that, I shall endeavor to pay you a visit at Berkley Square and lend a hand in the decoration plans." He gave her a probing look. "I most fervently hope you *have* decided to go ahead with renovations. The house is positively a tomb!"

Allegra threw an uneasy glance at her husband, wondering how he would react to his cousin's slur. His face displayed only amused tolerance, so she said, "One room at a time, perhaps. We could start with the music room. The wall panels are sadly tarnished and the parquet full of pits and cracks."

Percy went into raptures at the promise of advising Allegra on the choice of materials, decorative paper, and new paint. "Mind you, it is your decisions that count in the end, Allegra, but I shall be there to give you gentle nudges in the right direction."

"I wish I had your impeccable taste, Percy," Allegra said dryly.

"Not all members are gifted with such talent, yet we must stand together in important decisions," Percy replied seriously as if they were talking about selling the Berkley Square mansion rather than refurbishing it.

The drizzle slowly let up, clouds moving east and setting free the imprisoned sun. Allegra's heart lightened with Percy's nonsensical prattle and the merging sunshine. Down at the Reservoir they encountered two riders they knew, Lord Lewington and Justine Bryerly. Allegra flinched as she laid eyes on Justine, and her spirits were in an instant beleaguered with worry.

This won't do. I shan't let Wyndham's past affect me even if he hasn't forgotten Justine, she told herself. *Justine was once my friend, and nothing has really changed.* Filled with apprehension, she watched as the earl bowed over Justine's begloved hand. He held it longer than necessary, evidently unable to relinquish his hold. Allegra clutched the locket with the four-leaf clover attached to her bodice, but she feared her luck was on the wane, had been since the moment she stepped into Wyndham's coach that fatal dawn six weeks ago.

Allegra suppressed an urge to separate Justine and her husband by driving her horse like a wedge between them. She smiled and nodded as if nothing but the lovely morning and her ride mattered.

Lord Lewington, dark of hair and eye, was a tall, muscular gentleman with a wicked grin. He sat his black stallion in style, and Allegra realized why Justine had fallen for his easy charm and elegant form. He could set any lady's heart aflutter with his lazy eyes, but he showed no more interest in Allegra than she in him. A Bryerly groom rode beside Justine to lend respectability to the outing.

"Justine," the earl greeted smoothly. "Your eyes sparkle with zest this morning. I take it you did not dance all night long with this bounder." He indicated Lewington with the handle of his crop, and the marquess laughed derisively.

"I danced but the customary two dances with Lewington," Justine said stiffly. "And you should know better than to suggest that I acted improperly in any way."

The longing in Justine's eyes was evident as she regarded Lewington from under lowered lashes.

"As you well know, Wyndham, I don't care overly for dancing. Fencing is more my style," Lewington said.

"And *wenching*," Percy said *sotto voce*.

Allegra watched Justine, noting the desperate adoration in her friend's smile. All was not right in that direction, Allegra thought, feeling a spurt of compassion for the impetuous and headstrong Justine. She beckoned with her hand. "Come, ride with me. Let's leave the gentlemen to discuss their particular matters among themselves."

Justine shrugged delicately, casting a lingering glance at Lewington. "I daresay discussions of cockfights and horse racing are more of interest to our escorts than the latest news." Justine pulled up beside Allegra, and they set their mounts to a leisurely walk. "Did you know that Felicia Stanton—a member of our class at the academy—has married a duke thrice her age?"

Justine's smile held a brittle quality, and Allegra wondered if Wyndham's appearance had brought on that expression. "No, I didn't. As you well know, I can't attend any functions until I've been presented at a Drawing Room."

"A dead bore, isn't it?"

Allegra glanced into Justine's bright blue eyes, reading the pain. "Are you feeling quite the thing, Justine?"

"You should know that I—I don't love Wyndham," she blurted out, "never have. He's a dear, dear friend, but I can't, I never could *love* him. I jilted him because he's cold and cynical. I fear that no one will be able to break the wall around his heart, and it distresses me to see you in a position that will hurt you." She halted the rushed flow of her words. "Oh, I'm frightfully sorry. I didn't mean to imply— My tongue is running away with me—"

"If you don't love him, I suppose you did the right thing to cry off," Allegra interrupted, an uneasy feeling churning in her stomach. "He has, however, not forgotten you, I think." Her voice trembled on the last words, and she hated her weakness for the earl.

Justine turned her luminous eyes, darkened with worried questions, on Allegra. "Do you mind dreadfully that he—?"

"Is it so clear to you . . . is it written in my face—" Allegra could not finish the sentence.

"That you hold him in deep affection?" Justine filled in. "It's natural, I think. Wyndham is attractive, and such a commanding person. If my feelings had not been engaged elsewhere, I believe I might have lost my heart to Wyndham." She sighed deeply and placed a hand on Allegra's arm. "Forgive me for my frankness. I pray that we can remain friends, as always. Fate has played us a cruel trick, I think."

Allegra smiled through the pain that sat like a lump of ice in her chest. "Of course. I cherish your friendship— most of all your honesty. I don't blame you for the shattered state of Wyndham's heart."

Justine heaved a deep sigh. "Unfortunately I have no power to change—"

"No one can master his heart! He must come to grips with his life." Allegra forced a smile to her quivering lips. "I'm quite happy. I could not abide the thought of marrying Ezra Skelton, and the circumstances saved me from that fate. Besides, Wyndham is a true gentleman."

Justine turned in the saddle and looked at their escorts some distance away. "Yes . . . he is. He could have berated me, ranted and raved when I jilted him, but he only bowed and left the room."

"He grows pale when he's agitated, his eyes darken, and he sets his mouth into a thin line," Allegra said, and noticed the twinkle in her friend's eyes and the teasing smile.

"I declare you have memorized every detail of Wyndham's countenance."

"How very gauche of me," Allegra said flatly. "I should not wear my heart on my sleeve." She glanced toward the horizon, unable to shake off her growing feeling of gloom. "He will but scorn the weakness of my heart if he finds out. . . ."

Justine straightened her back and set her chin decisively. "You must not show him your true feelings. Let him believe that you're happy leading your own life." She smiled at Allegra. "I know you. He will be intrigued by your sparkling personality. Just don't let him see you wearing a Friday face. Nothing will more speedily push him away from home."

"You're very wise, Justine. Sometimes I believe you're so much older than your nineteen years."

"I don't care how old or wise I am if I cannot engage Lewington's affection. Without him the balls are dull, the musicales insipid, and the sumptuous dinners taste like shredded vellum." She took a deep breath and brushed her hand over her eyes. "No one has touched Lewington's heart, and I despair I never will. I'm only one of his many flirts."

The gentlemen rode up, and Justine wiped the hollow expression of grief off her face, replacing it with a fragile smile.

Allegra sensed her pain, and she could not resent Justine for being the keeper of Wyndham's affection. Allegra turned to her husband, only to see his gaze fixed upon the lady he could not have.

"I believe the rain will return shortly. I desire to return home, milord."

He jerked as if slapped and glanced at Allegra as if awakened from a dream. Her heart sank, and she couldn't bear to see the longing in his eyes.

"Certainly . . ." he said, unable to finish the sentence.

"Wyndham, why don't you accompany Justine and Lewington? I'm sure my discussions with Percy about refurbishing the house will bore you to flinders. Percy, would you like to take me home?" Without waiting for Wyndham's reply, she turned her mount toward the gate in the distance.

chapter 8

After the Court presentation, where Allegra wore a sumptuous hooped silk with a train, a diamond brooch that had belonged to the earl's mother, a diamond aigrette in her hair, and a fine ivory and chickenskin fan, she was pulled into a whirl of entertainment. Barely able to catch her breath, she went from ball to rout, from garden breakfast to masked balls. Sometimes the earl accompanied her, but more often she went with Percy and his mother, sometimes with Justine and her parents.

"You're wearing yourself to a shade, m'dear," said Percy one evening as he escorted her to the door of the Berkley Square mansion. "I've never known anyone to visit three balls in one evening. Before long you'll be no more than a gaunt shadow."

"That's as may be, but I am enjoying myself," Allegra said with a shaky smile, ignoring the pain in her heart. In an unceasing wave of activity she managed to forget that she had no one—not really—to whom she could confide her loneliness. She had come to loathe the moment she stepped into the door of the mansion, knowing that silence would close around her like a dense cocoon and the earl would not be there to greet her.

Lucy, of course, always waited up for her, and more often than not, Knocky would appear to inquire if she wanted him to run some errand. Staunch allies, Lucy and Knocky stood against the earl's indifference and wanted nothing more than to make Allegra happy. The other servants were slowly beginning to come around.

Percy took his leave, and Jasper, one of the burly footmen, closed the front door. Allegra went toward the stairs, her limbs dragging with fatigue. Out of the shadows cast by the oil lamps, Knocky's small form manifested.

"Melady, may I 'ave a word wi' ye afore ye step upstairs?"

She walked toward the boy, noting the friendly smile. "You are awake very late, Knocky. Is there a problem?"

"No ... melady, I couldn't be 'appier, seein' as I just 'ad a wedge of Cook's custard pie in th' larder." He lowered his voice and looked around. "But, melady, me 'ead is achin' something terrible, seein' as I'm not keen on thinkin' too 'ard. Which I 'ave been all day. There's a favor I owe a—two friends, y'see, a great spankin' favor."

Allegra stared in astonishment. She'd never seen Knocky preoccupied before. Actually, he was the most cheerful person she'd ever encountered. "You worry me. What could that be, pray tell?"

"Well, see, afore I came 'ere, I worked in many places, earnin' a farthin' 'ere, a shillin' there. I made friends wi' a set o' brothers, Xavier and Xerxes Rudd. Large as behemoths—one at least—but kindly as saints, melady. I think ye could use a set of footmen wot look substantial. And jest imagine 'ow well they would look on each side o' th' door, dressed the same. Yer guests would talk o' nothin' else. Ye'll be a success as a 'ostess." He tweaked his pointed chin as if pondering deeply. "I reckon a frolickin' do or somethin' would be just th' thing for this old 'ouse. Would liven it up. For that ye need more footmen."

Allegra thought about his suggestion, deciding it was a splendid idea. "I shall mention it to His Lordship. More than likely, he won't mind."

Knocky smiled his impish smile. "Wot 'bout Xavier and Xerxes, melady? Can they stay, then?"

Allegra stared in disbelief. "Are they here?"

"That they are. I stuffed 'em in me attic chamber, but they be angry as bears seein' as they don't fit too well in so small a room. I wouldn't want to kindle their wrath."

"I suppose not," Allegra said dryly. "Methinks you're taking many liberties in this house. How did you get them past Dogwood?"

"Well, in the afternoon, Dogwood takes forty winks in 'is pantry. Xavier and Xerxes might be giants, melady, but they walk no 'arder than a kitty. Nimble noddys, if ye want me opinion."

"Does His Lordship know about their presence?"

"No ... that 'e don't. Ye're th' one wot 'ires the staff, and a word in yer ear is wot I desired afore approachin' 'Is Lordship."

Allegra sighed and dragged her cashmere shawl on the floor as she headed up the stairs. "I suppose I shouldn't ask what favor you owe the Rudds?"

Knocky shifted on his nimble feet. "Naw, but that I'd be eternally grateful if ye could find a place fer 'em 'ere. They are 'ard up at the moment, and I wouldn't want to see 'em suffer. Or starve."

"That would be unthinkable," Allegra said and rolled her eyes. "Very well, I shall interview them tomorrow morning. Until that time, you'll have to keep them in your room."

"*Melady!* Where am I ter sleep? Ye don't know 'ow big these lobcocks are. I'll be trampled t' death in me own bed!"

"That's a risk you will have to take, Knocky. You brought this upon yourself. Good night."

When Wyndham came downstairs the next morning, he found two hulking men—one enormous, one tall and thin—in his hallway. They wore threadbare fustian coats, grimy neckerchiefs, gray linen, and breeches that held more darned patches than actual material. The most characteristic features in their good-natured faces were their strange pointed beards—a family trait no doubt—and bulbous noses, shiny from much rubbing. Four small eyes blinked with embarrassment, and big if nimble hands twiddled with hats of indeterminate color.

Noticing from the corner of his eye that Knocky was slinking down the corridor as fast as his short legs could carry him, the earl shouted,

"Return this instant, Knocky!"

The page slunk back into the hallway, his body poised as if ready for flight. "Ye wanted me, melord?" he asked, making big innocent eyes.

Wyndham placed his hands behind his back and fixed Knocky with a hard stare. "I want an explanation for this. Why are these men kicking their heels in my foyer?"

"Melady says they were to stay fer an interview." He introduced, "Xavier and Xerxes Rudd, former magicians of a travelin' theater, an' now destitute. Seekin' employment, melord." Knocky tried to look important but failed. His gaze slunk behind the earl and upward, a wide smile splitting his face as Allegra descended the stairs.

The earl could have shaken the page until his teeth rattled. He folded his arms over his chest and made himself ready for battle. His wife was not going to fill the mansion with all sorts of riffraff, not if she set any store by his opinion and—approval. He studied her face, so sweet and innocent, until her eyes laid eyes on the two strangers.

"Oh," she said, clapping a hand to her mouth. "I didn't realize they were *that* bi—impressive." She noticed him and stiffened. His heart softened a notch as fear replaced the sweet expression on her face. Her blue eyes widened, and her cheeks paled. Did he intimidate her so?

"Good morning," she uttered tonelessly. "You are abroad early, my lord."

He inserted a finger under the cravat to ease its tight starchy grip, then steeled himself against the part of him that was touched by his young bride. "It is fortunate that I am, lest Knocky would invite the entire population of London to admire our silver."

"Surely ... his two friends are most trustworthy, my lord. Knocky assured me—"

The earl gave Knocky's impish expression a baleful stare. "Be that as it may. Knocky has no authority here."

"Melady, I'm only tryin' to ape after yer deep sense of charity," Knocky said in injured tones. "Xavier and Xerxes are me friends an' in need of 'elp. They wouldn't dream of 'armin' a 'air on Yer Ladyship's 'ead." He addressed the earl. "Would be perfect footmen, melord. They 'ave 'eight and noble presence."

"Can they speak?" Wyndham inquired scathingly.

The burly fellow took a step forward and bowed reverently. "I be Xavier Rudd," he said, "an' this is me bruther, Xerxes, named o' the king of Persia wot invaded Greece. I'm named for Saint Francis Xavier, missionary. Our father was dotty 'bout 'istrionics."

"History, you mean," Allegra said with a grin.

"But a saint you are not," the earl pointed out in a tone of voice that implied the man hailed rather from the Nether regions of the Universe than the Upper.

"No, my lord. Only a magician wot traveled wi' a circus. Th' owner died, an' the artists 'ad to leave." He flexed muscular arms. "We're good, 'ardworking fellows, my lord."

Wyndham sighed and looked at his wife. "I doubt we need any more servants, Allegra." Under her disappointed scrutiny and the resigned expressions of the men, his resolve not to hire any footmen weakened. "Dogwood would hand in his notice, and *that* I do not want. He's served the Roydens all his life."

" 'E will 'avta abide wi' yer decision, melord," Knocky was quick to point out.

Allegra inserted, "I suppose we could hire them temporarily until our ball next month. Dogwood is bound to need help from as many footmen as he can find. They might as well start now."

The earl glanced at her compassionate expression and swore silently. "Is your heart set on this, Allegra?"

"We can't very well throw them out into the street to starve."

"Big youths like these would have no difficulty finding employment," he pointed out gently.

"They are asking for employment here, my lord."

Wyndham heaved a deep sigh of defeat. "Very well, we'll take them on for now, and after the ball, we'll see."

The large fellows grinned from ear to ear and slapped each other's backs. The earl addressed Xavier. "Since your name is so like your brother's, we'll call you Francis from now on." He turned to Knocky. "You'll be out on your ear after the ball if you don't behave. Dogwood has complained again about your singing on the top of your voice while at work."

"Better than cryin', melord," Knocky said and rocked on his heels. "That old gabey 'as no ear fer good music."

Allegra frowned at the youth. "You cannot call Dogwood a 'gabey,' Knocky. He is your superior, and you must obey him at all times. That's the end of it."

The earl chuckled and shook his head in disbelief. He offered her his arm on the way to the breakfast parlor. "Where did you learn such a cant expression for fool, my dear?"

"I didn't know the meaning, but I suspect it had a negative connotation. I'm sorry if I upset the order of the house."

"When we married, I bestowed all my worldly goods upon you, my wife. You have the right to choose your servants, but I suspect the Rudds are a pair of vagabonds."

"They seemed utterly harmless to me, my lord. They have kind faces and sweet eyes."

"If the silver and the finest china have disappeared with Knocky and the Rudds on the morrow, you shall have to eat your words."

"I'd much rather have breakfast," she said with a pert smile.

Allegra looked charming in a plain white cambric gown and a green gauze shawl embroidered with flowers slung over her shoulders. She touched a locket pinned to her bodice, and he'd noticed that she wore the trinket every day, fingering it often as if to seek reassurance. He had an urge to ask her about it but felt that they were not on such intimate footing as to broach such a personal subject.

The realization startled him. After all, they met every morning over breakfast, but he knew very little about her, about her preferences and dislikes. She'd proved to be vastly more observant about his habits. Hadn't she arranged for boiled eggs instead of the glue usually served? She always made sure that the dishes served were to his liking, and that Oglesby—who easily forgot details—always saw to polishing his shoes and boots to a mirrorlike shine.

He sensed the care, the compassion with which she did everything. Taking a good look at himself over the perfectly boiled egg, he felt like a complete coxcomb, who could not get beyond his own broken heart and value the lady he had right by his side.

Visions of Justine smiling, Justine laughing and crying, Justine talking animatedly filled him, and however much he tried, he could not push the vivid pictures away. Loathing himself for his weakness, he could not dispel the haunting memories of his former love.

"You're in a brown study this morning, my lord. Is there something I can do to help? Are you upset about the new servants?" his wife asked softly. He glanced into her lovely earnest eyes, and suspected he was the lowest cad alive.

"No . . . but thank you for caring. I was only thinking of a problem that has nothing to do with the servant situation."

"I wouldn't want to go against your wishes in anything," she whispered and bent down to retrieve her napkin which had fallen to the floor. She blushed and fumbled with the reticule resting beside her plate.

"My lord—" she said in a breathless voice.

"I wish you would call me Ian," he said with some sharpness.

"Ian . . ." She lowered her thick, curling lashes and blushed even more deeply. To think that he'd never noticed the lovely feminine detail of her lashes before. "I hope you won't mind, but I've bought something, a nonsensical trinket for you." Her hands trembled as she grappled with the cord holding the reticule opening together. "A trifle really."

With a wobbly smile, she placed a round smooth form with a silvery sheen in his palm. "A snuffbox! How very kind. The enameling on the lid is superb."

"It depicts a falconry scene from Yorkshire, I believe. The Dales—remind me of our hon—*trip* north." She gasped and spoke quickly. "You see, the proprietor of the shop—" Her voice petered out. "I remembered that you like the Dales' scenery."

"I do! But it is not my birthday, nor is it a day for special celebration. Why waste your funds on exquisite trifles like this?"

"Well, I thought you would be pleased. I happened upon it," she added hastily, as if to emphasize that she'd acted impulsively, not planned to bestow an expensive gift upon him.

"I treasure it. In fact, I shall pour some of my favorite blend in it presently. I pray you won't spend all your pin money. . . ?"

"Do not worry about me, my lord—Ian." She looked away, a shadow a discomfort passing across her face. Possessed with an uneasy feeling, he yearned to question her if she needed more money besides her quarterly allowance, but something in him held back. He didn't feel comfortable enough to question her personal habits, and let the query slide away from his mind. If only—

A knock sounded on the door, and Dogwood entered, closely followed by Percy Harcombe. Wyndham swore silently as the moment of intimacy slipped away. The snuffbox felt as round and smooth as her cheek, and he would have to be content with touching the polished silver.

"No need to stand on ceremony, Dogwood," Percy said. "Good morning all," he said cheerfully and lifted the lids of the silver dishes on the sideboard. "Is there some kedgeree left? I'm famished." Without an invitation he sat down by the table and looked from host to hostess.

"What is the matter? You both look ill at ease, and Friday-faced. Did I interrupt a salacious argument?"

"Perce, you're becoming more rude every day. Have you no sense of delicacy?" The earl eyed his cousin with misgiving, taking note of the waistcoat in violent shades of green and yellow. "I grow quite bilious staring at your waistcoat so early in the morning."

"Balderdash! People expect a certain style. I can't very well venture outside and ruin everyone's expectations."

"A subtle stripe would be more the thing, coz."

Dogwood refilled their cups and placed a serving of toast and kedgeree before Percy, who rubbed his hands in anticipation.

"Who are those tall ruffians in the hallway? I thought I was seeing double, and, as far as I know, there ain't anything wrong with my eyes. Nor did I look too deeply in the brandy bottle last night, not deeply enough to give me distorted vision."

Allegra pressed her fingertips to her mouth, but a chuckle escaped nevertheless. "Your expression provoked my mirth, Percy. The new footmen—Francis, the burly one, and Xerxes, the thin one. I just hired them this morning."

Percy wore a perplexed expression. "The peculiar thing is that I gave one of them my hat, but when I turned around, the other fellow was holding it. I did the same with my walking stick, and it disappeared right in front of my eyes. I daresay I am ready for Bedlam."

"Hmmm," Wyndham said, wishing he could flay Knocky's backside for bringing such scaly fellows into the house. Still, however exasperating Knocky was, the imp served his mistress cheerfully and kept her in good spirits. "Mayhap you are, Perce. Come to think of it, anyone who wears a waistcoat like yours is a Bedlamite. I shall have one of the new footmen escort you back there posthaste."

"Your glee is nauseating, Ian, but I declare you won't laugh so smugly once your valuables start disappearing."

Allegra said, "I shall rig out Francis and Xerxes in livery and see to it that they wear powdered wigs when they have duty by the door. It wouldn't do to send our female guests into a swoon at their raffish appearance."

"Mark my words, you and your new servants will be the talk of London before the day is over," Percy said matter-of-factly.

"Oh? Are you going to spread the rumor that we have hired two magicians to guard our door?" the earl asked and laughed. He caressed the old snuffbox in his hand, its smoothness as velvety as the inside skin of Allegra's wrist. The thought made him strangely happy. He threw her a quick glance to see if she'd noticed his fascination with the snuffbox, but she was only laughing at one of Percy's sallies. Her eyes sparkled, remarkably pretty when she laughed, he thought.

"I daresay your taste in servants is highly irregular," Percy declared and picked at the food. He threw longing glances at the steaming slabs of ham on the sideboard.

"Is something wrong with your appetite, coz?" the earl asked.

"No . . . but I have to be strong, resist the temptations of my greedy appetite. Otherwise, I will die a bachelor."

"Pish! You're much to plump in the pocket for that, Perce. If nothing else, you'll get leg-shackled to someone who falls in love with your blunt." The earl realized the coldness of that reply and threw a glance at his wife across the table. Her gaze darted away, but he'd seen the stricken look and the nervous flutter of her hands on the teacup.

"Blunt ain't everything in life," Percy said and smiled at Allegra. "I'd like to find someone as personable as your wife. You are a lucky beggar, Ian."

Uncomfortable silence hung in the room, and a wave of shame went through Wyndham. He couldn't feel the honor of being married to Allegra, only the burden of having wed a lady he did not love. Marriage to Justine would have been so very different. His heart would have been engaged even if their wills had clashed. He knew they would have argued, but with love to soften their disagreements, life would have been so much more exciting, more rewarding than it was under the current circumstances.

He berated himself for his churlishness, for his inability to forget a love that might have been doomed from the start, for his difficulty to wholly accept Allegra's presence at his side and at his table. He caressed the smooth surface of the snuffbox and pondered the thoughtfulness that had prompted her to purchase the gift for him.

Allegra took notice of the subtle movement of Wyndham's hand on her gift and was ridiculously pleased that she'd found something he truly liked. Perhaps she would find a way to his heart if she could stretch her patience. To buy the snuffbox had been an act of impulse which had depleted her funds disastrously. Somehow money seemed to slip through her fingers like water.... But a gift? She couldn't resist. No need to worry about that now, she thought, squirming. Her reverie was interrupted as Dogwood came into the room and shut the door with unusual vehemence.

She looked at his red face and furious eyes. "Oh, dear, what is wrong, Dogwood?"

He bowed to Allegra, then addressed the earl. "I know I should not trouble you, my lord, but I have a matter of the gravest urgency to discuss with you."

The earl leaned back in his chair and slipped the snuffbox into his pocket. "What in the world has put you in high dudgeon, Dogwood?"

"I'm afraid I will have to speak with you in private, my lord."

The singing voice of a cherub could be heard drifting from the far-off music room. "Are you upset with Knocky again?" Allegra asked, understanding from whose mouth the singing had erupted.

"Not only *that*," blurted Dogwood, "but there are two hideous *persons* in the music room with him. They look dangerous, if I may be so bold."

Allegra hid a smile behind her hand. The earl sighed deeply, chagrin written across his face. Percy craned his neck as far as his high shirtpoints would allow.

"He means the two ruffians, no doubt," Percy said.

"They are not ruffians, but magicians," Allegra explained, and Dogwood gasped. His eyes bulged with shock, and he took a step back.

"Dear me, they will spirit away everything of value in this house!" he screeched. "I shall have the entire staff of footmen show the persons to the door immediately."

"Not a successful strategy, I'm afraid," the earl drawled, his lips twitching with amusement. "They will only point out that we hired them. Francis and Xerxes Rudd are our new footmen, Dogwood. I would appreciate it if you would see to ordering livery that is large enough for their tall frames."

"What is the world coming to?" Dogwood muttered and wrung his hands. "I'm overset with this turn of events. I would have thought you would be very particular whom—" He stopped abruptly, evidently realizing he was overstepping his shackles. "Ruffians," he muttered under his breath. "*Barbarians!* I daresay I will have to hand in my notice," he added stiffly.

"This is the second time you've threatened to leave us, Dogwood." The earl pressed his fingertips together. "There's one detail I would like to stress before you leave, namely that Her Ladyship was kind enough to hire your relative Lucy as her personal maid. That was far higher a station than what could have been expected for such a ... *spirited* ... young person as Lucy."

Dogwood cleared his throat and inserted a finger under his starched collar. "I daresay it was a great favor to my family."

"Am I correct to surmise that you're no longer as eager to leave your employ as you were a minute ago?" Wyndham asked subtly, and Allegra admired him for his cool control. No problem seemed too large or too overwhelming for him to tackle. "Just remember the advantage to your family supplied by you and Lucy."

Dogwood hemmed and hawed, but Allegra noticed the subdued expression taking precedence over the anger. "I suppose I could not find a better position at this time," the butler said haughtily.

"I'm sure you will get along well with Francis and Xerxes. They seem good-natured enough. And remember, you'll never have to lift anything heavy again with those two—especially Francis—in the house."

Dogwood bowed and said in funereal tones, "I will see to their new livery, my lord."

Relief and pleasure washed through Allegra as she listened to Ian deal with the butler. She was grateful that he'd chosen to take her side. Possibly Francis and Xerxes would end up stealing something of value and slink away, but the earl had chosen to humor her whim, to trust her judgment. The knowledge warmed her heart. "Well, I wouldn't want the fellows to starve," she said mostly to herself.

"See what I mean, Ian?" Percy said. "She has the softest heart of anyone I've ever known."

Wyndham scrutinized her, his gaze digging into her soul for that sweetness. Could he see it, she wondered, or did he only see her as a weight upon his shoulders?

chapter 9

Percy came six mornings in a row to help Allegra choose the fabric for the wall panels, the curtains, and the upholstery in the music room. What had previously been red brocade panels now became gold watered silk. The furniture got dressed in thin stripes of gold and moss green, and the drapes framed the windows with sumptuous folds of pale gold velvet held back with tassels. For all his flamboyant taste in clothing, Percy showed an impeccable taste in home decor. "Invite warmth, cheer up this tomb," were words he used over and over as he relegated musty drapes and looming pieces of furniture to the attic (carried there by Francis and Xerxes).

As Allegra and Percy, one week after Dogwood's outburst, admired the newly polished sheen of the pianoforte, and the bright swirling pattern of the Axminster carpet, the earl joined them in the music room. He looked around, his eyebrows raised in surprise.

"By Jove, I think this is a great improvement! I'm tempted to spend some time in this cheerful chamber, reading, or"—his lips quivered—"listening to Knocky's angelic singing."

Allegra had an idea. "Why not send out invitations for

a musicale? A small gathering of people, a buffet, nothing elaborate. Our friends only."

"Yes . . . that would be pleasurable, more so than the tedious ball looming ahead."

Allegra sat down an hour later to write invitations for an informal musicale a week hence. Knowing that most of her acquaintances would be engaged to attend other functions, she only sent out invitations to her friends and closest relatives, including Justine Bryerly. Tears gathered into her eyes as she wrote the name on the envelope and sealed it with wax. Perhaps Justine's love for Lord Lewington would so disgust Wyndham that his heart would heal. It was a gamble, but Allegra felt she would gain nothing by trying to keep them apart. They were bound to meet at other balls and functions.

The night of the musicale arrived, Allegra's first gathering as hostess of the Berkley Square mansion. She came downstairs wearing a narrow mauve silk shift covered with a half-length tunic of gold net and cut in a daring neckline. A thin chain of sapphires around her neck and an elaborate coiffure of curls held together over her ears with jeweled combs completed her toilette.

"Yer eyes sparkle like jools, an' the fancy 'air arrangement makes ye look years older, me lady. You've never looked better. 'Is Lordship's bound to take notice and be that proud," Knocky commented in the hallway.

Allegra's heart warmed, and she wondered if her husband would seek her later in her bedchamber. He had not visited her since their disastrous honeymoon, and she feared he now despised and abhorred the thought of approaching her again. If anything, she lived in fear of the moment when he would return to claim his right, but at the same time his indifference slighted her.

She came eye to eye with Francis and Xerxes, who looked uncomfortable in their stiff new livery. "Just remember to take the guests' hats and outer garments and deposit them upstairs in one of the guest chambers."

"Yes, melady," said Francis, the talkative one. Xerxes barely ever said a word, only nodded and smiled shyly. The household was in upheaval due to the two tricksters. They would pluck potatoes from Leon's pockets and eggs from Dogwood's hair. It almost seemed as if they could spirit away people, because Knocky was never to be found when he was most needed. When not employed running errands, the three servants were inseparable.

"Your powdered wigs look splendid," Allegra said.

"But they itch arful. I never took to 'orse 'air, melady."

"You'll get used to it. Go stand outside the door and bow to all the guests before you let them in." She inspected their spotless gloves and glanced at their stockings for holes or tears, then sent them to their posts. Was her husband ready to take his stance by her side?

The earl watched her from the top of the stairs and listened to her tinkling laugh as she motioned the footmen out the door. A balmy breeze caressed the night, and stars glittered in the sky, a perfect night to introduce a small gift to his skittish wife. He strolled downstairs while touching the narrow flat case in his pocket. Her eyes widened in surprise—or was it pleasure?—as she noticed his presence. Those bright blue eyes had begun to insinuate themselves into his thoughts.

"Allegra, my dear, would you inspect the music room with me before the guests arrive?" he asked smoothly and held out his arm for her.

She accepted, and he sensed the tension in her body as they walked into the chamber that would hold their guests.

"Is there something wrong?" she asked.

"No, not at all. I would like to give you something."

The music room had been filled with rows of gilt chairs, and besides the pianoforte, violins waited for their owners, who were imbibing ale and eating a light repast in the servants' dining room. "You have managed to make this room very inviting, Allegra. In fact, you have brought life into this mansion, and I am eternally grateful. Even the servants are friendlier."

She blushed and looked down at the tips of her slippers. "Thank you, Ian. I'll try to make this evening a grand success. The buffet has been arranged in the drawing room and the tables set up in the garden with colored lanterns."

"Splendid." He lifted her chin with one hand and hauled out the case with the other. "Here's a bauble I picked up at Rundell and Bridge. They are also resetting the Wyndham Diamonds into a necklace that is to come into your possession shortly."

He watched her flushed face as she opened the case and saw the bracelet of small sapphires, like those around her neck. A larger square-cut gem formed the clasp. She gasped.

"This is lovely, Ian! Can I wear it tonight?"

He smiled, a warm feeling invading his chest. "Of course you may. Do you have to ask?"

"I . . . it's too much. You didn't have to exert yourself in this fashion."

He held up the bracelet and lifted her arm. The subtle perfume of her skin reached his nose, and he inhaled deeply, savoring the fragrance. He could not explain the novel sensation of humble warmth in his heart. The experience had a wholly different flavor than his desperate love for Justine Bryerly. With her, he'd felt a need to conquer, to storm, to tame. A desperate passion that needed to be fulfilled. Allegra invoked care, a need to protect and cherish. Was it perhaps only a brotherly concern for her welfare? Yes, that must be what he was feeling tonight. Yet . . . yet the skin on the inside of her wrist was so desperately soft.

He undid the clasp of the thin row of sapphires and draped them around her arm. He fastened it and patted her hand. "That's it. Let's see how it looks." He pulled out her arm, tilting it back and forth, and her gaze searched his face. "Lovely," he said, swallowing the lump in his throat.

Allegra's lips had a lost, vulnerable look, and her eyes were deep pools of yearning. Could it be? No ... he said to himself, she was too young to know the depths of love. He leaned forward, mesmerized by the soft plumpness of her lips.

"Thank you," she whispered, "there was no need to give me anything."

Torn from the spell of the moment, he straightened his back. With difficulty did he manage to pull himself out of the seductive trance.

"No need to thank me, Allegra. You are my wife, and as such are entitled to the finest jewelry available. The sapphires look superb."

Allegra went to the girandole mirror hanging beside the fireplace and held up her wrist so that the bracelet rested close to the necklace. The jewels glowed like chips of blue ice against her white skin. "Very tasteful. How did you know it would match my necklace?"

Wyndham smiled. "Lucy was gracious enough to permit me a quick peek into your jewelry case. I am rather good at sketching, so I brought a picture of your necklace to the jeweler."

"How clever," was all Allegra could think of saying.

They stared at each other for a long moment, tension tightening with the stretching silence.

"I suppose it's time to meet our guests," he said hoarsely and opened the door for her.

As they waited in the hallway, the earl asked, "By the way, whom did you hire to sing?"

"La Naldi. She's known to be temperamental. I hope she won't arrive late."

As Allegra finished speaking, the front door opened and Giles Temple stormed into the house. "Sis, by God, who are those *bearded* fellows?" he asked in a loud whisper as they embraced.

"My new footmen. Don't you like them?" Allegra laughed, thrilled to see that her brother had accepted her invitation. "How long will you stay, Giles? Do you have to go back to Oxford immediately?"

"We'll talk about that later," Giles replied from the side of his mouth. He threw a glance of apprehension at the earl's stern countenance. "Need to see you alone, sis."

A shiver of premonition traveled up Allegra's spine. Giles was in trouble, as much was clear. She viewed his flamboyant dress of yellow unmentionables, a green brocaded waistcoat that would have looked better as a chair cover, and a blue coat with extravagant buttons. She wished he would take note of Wyndham's discreet attire of dark blue coat and gray pantaloons and use him as a model for good taste. She noticed from the corner of her eye, however, that her husband repeatedly tried to ease the folds of his neckcloth. Too much starch.

"There are Aunt Irene and Lydia Sinclair," Giles said and swept his aunt into an excessive embrace. She chuckled and begged to be set down.

Lydia pecked Allegra's cheek and gave her a mischievous smile. "You look stunning. The new hair arrangement, and those *sapphires*, make you look quite grown up and elegant. I've never seen you so glowing."

Allegra's spirits soared, and she regarded her husband with hope. Perhaps Wyndham would come to see her as a desirable lady, not as his younger sister. *Desirable!* The word made her realize she would then have to accept his advances. The thought made her stiff with apprehension. If only she knew what to expect from him.

More guests welled into the house, most of them expressing awe at Francis and Xerxes, who had gathered an enormous pile of hats and outer garments and were carrying the tower upstairs. "I swear one of them took my beaver," Percy said upon arrival, "and the other one had it in his hand a mere second later. Even though I stared most closely, I did not see the first one—the thin one—hand over my hat. Most confounding."

Allegra laughed. "You've always received the right hat back upon leaving this house, haven't you?"

"Yes." Percy rubbed his chin. "I daresay they are entertaining fellows, if a trifle intimidating. Their remarkable size, y' know."

Justine Bryerly and her mother, escorted by Lord Lewington, arrived among the last. Allegra knew when they entered by the stiffening of Wyndham's shoulders. She peeped around his tall form to confirm her suspicion as to the identity of the pair. Lewington looked splendid in a charcoal-gray coat and gray trousers. Justine, as an unmarried young lady in her second season in town, wore a simple white muslin dress, a fringed Norwich shawl slung from elbow to elbow, and a painted fan in her gloved hand. Her vivacious face glowed and her sable curls bounced as she greeted Allegra.

"Thank you for inviting me. I do adore to hear La Naldi sing." She leaned closer and whispered, "To be seen with Wyndham like this will stop some of the nasty rumors that he's still wearing the willow for me. Really, he looks totally unconcerned and gave me the *coldest* of looks."

All to hide his true feelings, Allegra thought. "That ought to silence some of the tattlemongers."

"You have such a level head on your shoulders, Allegra,

such composure. To face a loveless marriage would kill me."

"Balderdash. It happens all the time." *I will be destroyed bit by bit if Wyndham doesn't change,* Allegra added silently.

The guests trooped into the music room, many exclaiming over the lovely new decor. Percy preened, absorbing the compliments as if he alone had transformed the room.

Allegra spoke to Dogwood. "I'm worried. Has La Naldi arrived yet?"

Dogwood shook his head morosely. "No, but mark my words, she'll be exceptionally late. Always is."

Anxious, she commanded the footmen to carry around glasses of refreshment while the guests waited for the opera singer to arrive. She caught Wyndham's gaze across the room, and he lifted his eyebrows in inquiry. She shook her head, feeling ridiculously inadequate. What if the evening—her first entertainment—turned into a complete fiasco?

Clammy with worry, she waited an hour later for the tardy singer. The noise of the guests had taken on a peevish note, and Allegra realized they would not wait much longer. She hovered in the hallway, too worried to keep up a conversation.

Finally a servant came to the back door with a message. Dogwood bore it to Allegra, and she broke the seal with trembling fingers. "My goodness!" she exclaimed as she read the lines. "La Naldi has lost her voice! She's in the miserable depths of a head cold." Allegra tossed the missive back to Dogwood. "This is a disaster. Why didn't she write me earlier? Whatever shall I do?"

"You must devise some other entertainment, my lady."

Allegra tried to gather her wits. "I don't play the pianoforte well. Besides, I wouldn't want to push my poor talents on my esteemed guests."

"Miss Bryerly has an excellent singing voice," Dogwood said.

Allegra spirits sank. Justine's sweet voice would surely impress Wyndham's already smitten heart. "Yes . . . yes, of course, I do remember that she's sings superbly."

Allegra went into the music room, where the clamor had risen to a fever pitch. She swallowed hard and stepped up to the podium, where the pianoforte waited with its empty bench. The two violinists moved uneasily on their spindly chairs.

"Dear guests," Allegra began, "I'm distressed to inform you that La Naldi is indisposed and won't be able to entertain us tonight."

Whispers moaned across the room, and Allegra waited until everyone returned their attention to her. "I beg of you to stay and later partake of the buffet. I know we have great talents among ourselves and would dearly like to hear some music." She glanced at Justine, who grimaced. Allegra pleaded with her eyes, and Justine rose reluctantly, putting her fan aside. "Miss Bryerly sings exceptionally well, and her skill at the pianoforte is unmatched."

Justine smiled and studied the music sheets, then conferred with the violinists. Drawing a sigh of relief, Allegra sat down on a chair just below the dais. Lewington got up and offered to turn the music sheets.

The room filled with silent expectation. Justine's voice soon wafted, high and pure, to the ceiling, and Allegra could not help but send surreptitious glances at Wyndham, whose gaze was riveted to Justine's animated features. His face held no expression, but Allegra knew that deep emotion for Justine still flowed in his veins. Lewington wore an amused smile, and Allegra wondered if Justine had managed to secure his love. Who could withstand Justine's charming allure? She glanced up at the marquess with her heart in her eyes.

Justine ended with a popular *chanson*, its melancholy tune entrancing the audience.

"Bravo!" cried Percy as the song ended, and the guests applauded enthusiastically.

Allegra wondered who to nudge into singing next. Aunt Irene beckoned her from the first row of seats. "Lydia and I could sing a duet if you like. It should round out the music evening," she whispered in Allegra's ear.

"Thank you! I can't stress enough how grateful I am. You're saving me from disaster." She got up on the dais and announced the next entertainers, then left the room to inquire if the buffet was ready.

She closed the door behind her and went in search of Dogwood. Footmen scurried back and forth with trays, and Knocky transported a case of bottles into the drawing room. "Fill some glasses and offer the guests, Knocky, as soon as the entertainment is over. The footmen can help you."

"My lady!" cried Dogwood and hurried over as fast as his stiff legs could carry him. "It's raining outside, positively a downpour."

Allegra clapped her hands to her cheeks. "Not this! I am already struggling to keep the entertainment together." She went to the window and stared at the dismal weather outside. "We will have to bring in the tables."

"There are too many guests to fit into one room."

"What about the dining room?"

"My lady, the workers have begun repairs. The wall panels are all gone."

"Whatever shall I do?" She went into the drawing room and surveyed the heap of tablecloths that Mrs. Buxton and the maids had arranged in one corner.

"They are somewhat damp, my lady," the housekeeper said. "The rain came on very quickly."

"I wanted the effect of a picnic," Allegra wailed and

looked at the drooping lanterns strung among the trees. A candle went out with a hiss. Rain lashed the terrace, and the garden was a dripping green grotto, dismal in its cold wetness.

Allegra stared at the empty expanse of carpet in the drawing room. She had a wild idea. "Mrs. Buxton! Carry all the pillows you can find in the house and disperse around tablecloths on the floor. We shall have an indoor picnic."

"I've never heard of such a harebrai—such an idea before," Mrs. Buxton said loftily.

"Dogwood will arrange the whole to look like a picnic—plates, baskets of bread, bottles on ice. A candelabrum in the middle of each tablecloth, please. The footmen will move around the room with platters of food."

"Highly irregular," Dogwood muttered and gave her a sour glance. " 'Tis scandalous, and we don't have time—"

"Please do not linger. I shall stall the guests for another half hour." Allegra hurried back to the music room, unable to think of a single thing that would entertain her guests while the servants made the drawing room ready.

She opened the door, and a blast of laughter met her. To her surprise, Aunt Irene and Lydia had left the podium, and occupying it now were Knocky and the Rudd brothers. Allegra gasped and clutched the doorframe to keep herself from fainting with shock.

She frantically searched the throng for her husband, finding his gaze turned upon her. He shrugged and gave her an exasperated smile.

Knocky was playing the pianoforte with gusto and sang popular tunes in his angelic tenor voice. As he noticed Allegra, he gave her a merry wave, and Allegra could have strangled him with her bare hands at that moment.

Stricken with shock, however, she could only gape at the antics of the Rudds. Xerxes, the thin brother, was balancing on Francis's shoulders and juggling with five apples. His hands moved so quickly the apples appeared to be an unbroken wheel. Meanwhile, Francis was balancing on one leg, powdered wig askew, and making a copper coin disappear and appear from various parts of his anatomy.

The guests roared with laughter, and Allegra let herself be beguiled by the servants' impudent exhibition. If Dogwood saw this, he would surely hand in his notice.

Allegra had never heard of any hostess who had offered such common entertainment, and she wondered if she would be the laughingstock of London on the morrow.

Francis tossed up the coin, and Xerxes caught it with his mouth, letting the apples drop one after the other into his brother's waiting hands. Ooohs and aaahs rose to the ceiling, and Allegra realized that the guests enjoyed the entertainment immensely, all but the two violinists, who tried to shrink into the wall.

The guests' enjoyment, however, did not mean that scandal had been averted. Allegra prayed that she would be able to hold her head up in polite society after this night.

chapter 10

When Xerxes finally jumped down from his brother's shoulders, a wild applause rent the air. Standing by the door, Allegra drew a deep sigh of relief as she heard the cheers and laughter of the audience.

She tried to catch the earl's attention, but he was talking to Percy, his face expressionless. Allegra had learned that Wyndham was a master at concealing his true feelings behind a mask of polite indifference. At least Percy's face held an amused smile, and he gesticulated as if mimicking Xerxes juggling.

Aunt Irene bustled up, her face white with worry. "Oh, dear, Allegra. Did you plan for this bawdy romp to happen? It might have been too much for some of the older guests. Your name will be bandied about London by tomorrow."

"I did not plan it," Allegra said between clenched teeth as she watched Knocky strutting around talking to the guests as if he were the host and not a servant. "I think the fault lies with my page, who has no sense for propriety, and no respect."

"How cheeky. You must keep your servants in order, Allegra," Irene said with a sigh. "Performances like this will not do. You will be ruined."

"At least he did not sing ditties," Allegra said, furious with the audacious imp.

"Thank heaven for that!" Irene flapped her fan to cool her face. "I'd be mortified if this had happened in my house."

"Unusual entertainment ought not be frowned upon as long as it falls within the limits of good taste." Allegra searched desperately for her husband's support as the guests started rising from their seats. The earl was nowhere to be seen. She hurried up to the front of the room and called for attention.

"It's raining heavily outside, so I decided to move the *picnic* inside. The seating is not arranged by name." She quaked inside as she waited to hear the first expressions of outrage when the guests realized what kinds of "tables" she'd arranged in the drawing room. Inhaling deeply to support her composure, which that was threatening to dissolve, she ushered the guests through the hallway.

At first the guests fell into utter silence as they viewed the picnic in the drawing room. Then someone exclaimed, "Charming! How utterly original!"

Allegra recognized Justine's voice, and she silently blessed her friend. She prayed that the other guests' opinion would be swayed to favorably view the indoor picnic.

The guests swarmed through the room, clustering around the pillows and tablecloths in groups of five and six. For the elderly guests, Allegra had the footmen bring in chairs from the music room, but within minutes, most of the visitors were seated on the floor on plump cushions drinking champagne.

By Allegra's instruction, lackeys kept replenishing the glasses, wine her only hope that her guests would look upon her radical entertainment with mellow eyes and open minds. Where was Wyndham?

* * *

The earl leaned against the doorframe and stared at the spectacle in front of him. The room was swathed in darkness except for the light cast by the candles in the middle of each tablecloth. He'd never seen anything like it! Guests sprawled on the floor in all their finery, chatting and breaking bread. The footmen carried around platters of lobster patties, pâtés, glazed ham, jellies, cakes, and pastries. The guests helped themselves cheerfully from every platter as far as he could tell. It reminded him that he'd been joking with Allegra about a picnic at Newberry House—and here they were, picnicking in their own home.

"Capital entertainment," Percy said from the depth of a cushion at the first "table." He was foraging among the delicacies on his plate and offered the earl the empty pillow beside him. "Poor Allegra. I daresay she's worrying herself into a decline."

Wyndham looked for his wife and found her seated beside a formidable dowager. A rigid smile sat on her lips. He studied her closed face, sensing the terrible strain in her slender body. He squelched an urge to go to her side and encourage her. She might take offense, thinking his reassurance patronizing. He didn't know her well enough to gauge what her reaction would be. The realization shook him. Was he so self-absorbed that he failed to understand his wife's feelings?

Not that this gathering was less than an outrage, mayhap even a scandal, but he grudgingly recognized her effort to make a success of her first evening as hostess despite the heavy odds against her.

"I must say she shows bottom," he said, stroking his chin. At first he'd been aghast at the arrangements, but his sense of humor was soon tickled.

"She enlivens this gloomy house, doesn't she? A veritable ray of sunshine," Percy said and speared a sliver of ham with his fork. He stopped short of his mouth and put the fork down, then patted his middle surreptitiously. The earl sat down and raised his glass to the other guests around the tablecloth.

"She has brought a certain liveliness to this house," Wyndham said to Percy. "There has not been a moment of peace since the first moment I clapped eyes on her," he added, laughing. "Not only did she foist a needle-toed kitten upon me, but she managed to turn the entire household upside down."

"Allegra and her kitten are the best tenants you've ever had, Ian. Admit it."

"Well, they are tenants for life, aren't they?" A lady wearing a cluster of dyed ostrich feathers in her hair bent forward, lending an unobstructed view of his wife. Allegra happened to return his glance, and the whole room seemed to fade, guests becoming shadows. Her glance sent a shock through his body, and his breath caught in his throat.

Her cheerful presence in his life was slowly eroding the steel wall that surrounded his heart. Instead of feeling outrage at her actions, especially her hiring of eccentric servants, he felt his defenses weakening, laughter and disbelief taking their place. He'd never realized how much her humor and strange logic could warm his life.

Sighing, he lifted his glass toward her and bowed. To his delight, she blushed to the roots of her hair, and glanced away, a dazed expression on her face. She touched the ever present locket on her bodice as if distracted. He would have to find out what she was hiding there. The miniature of a youthful lover? The thought sent a spurt of corroding jealousy through his blood.

Allegra's heart filled with ridiculous happiness as the earl showed his approval, and her fear subsided. Her legs weakened at his smile. Thank God, she was sitting down—if on a very lumpy pillow. She glanced around the room for Knocky and the Rudd brothers, but they had disappeared after their impromptu performance. What they needed was a good tongue-lashing, and they knew they would receive one if they lingered in the house.

Too worried about the outcome of this unusual event, she didn't touch any of the delicacies on her plate. The evening dragged on interminably.

By the time the guests had departed, Allegra was ready to collapse into a heap on the hallway floor, but she gathered her wits and asked Dogwood for Knocky and the Rudds.

"They are gone out, milady," Dogwood said with a long-suffering air.

"I thought as much." Too tired to talk with anyone, she dragged herself up the stairs to Lucy's waiting presence.

"What a night. I'll never live through the wave of gossip that is bound to follow." She dropped onto the chair by the dressing table, and Lucy started brushing out Allegra's hair arrangement.

"Pooh. Ye might be the talk of the town by tomorrow, but mark me words, ye'll be famous for yer darin'."

"I'm not sure I want to be known for my *daring*," Allegra said darkly. "By the way, where are Knocky and the Rudds?"

Lucy's gaze flickered away. "I daresay they went out for a drop o' ale." She hesitated. "I'm supposed to let them back in when ever'one is asleep."

"His Lordship will take a strap to their backsides." Allegra leaned back in her chair, savoring the feel of the hairbrush against her aching scalp.

"Naw, I think 'Is Lordship is amused wi' their antics. Never been a quiet moment since that Knocky started workin' 'ere. Dogwood is that irritated with th' imp."

"Dogwood is not the only one."

Lucy twisted the long hair into a braid. "There."

Allegra stood and allowed her maid to unfasten her dress and pull off her silk stockings. Dressed in her nightgown, she sat down on the bed and patted Beau, who had made himself a nest among the pillows. "You slept through the debacle," she said to the kitten and scratched his chin.

Beau stretched to double length and dug his nails into the mattress. He looked at Allegra through slitted eyes and purred, rolling around in bliss.

Yawning hugely, Allegra said good night to her maid and lifted the top sheet to crawl under it. A soft knock came on the door to Wyndham's bedchamber. She stiffened, wondering if her husband had plans to give her a rakedown. He hadn't visited her bedroom since that first miserable night.

She feared his wrath, but politely asked him to enter.

"You look all done in, my dear," he said pleasantly. "Has it been a trying night?" He was wearing a dressing gown over shirt and breeches, and Allegra drew a sigh of relief. He hadn't come to repeat the fiasco of their wedding night. Yet, a sliver of disappointment lodged in her chest, and she wondered at her contrary reaction.

"I am tired, my lord—Ian." She caressed Beau as he strolled across the bed to investigate the intruder. He curled his tail around the bedpost and meowed.

Abstractedly the earl reached out to pet the furry head. His face set in stern lines, he pinned Allegra with his penetrating gaze.

She swallowed nervously. "Have you come to give me a beargarden jaw, Ian? I expect I deserve it, but please bear in mind that I was desperate to salvage the event somehow. Everything went wrong, as you well know."

"Percy fancied the picnic a great success, and I daresay Knocky has a fine singing voice. In fact, he has the makings of a splendid tenor."

"You're not angry with me?"

He shook his head and smiled. "No, I usually find the musicales a dead bore, but I can't recall a time when I've been more entertained."

Allegra laughed in great relief. "You're not going to fly into the boughs once the gossip reaches your ears tomorrow?"

"Gossip is like the wind—changes direction every day." He leaned against the bedpost, staring openly at her, and Allegra was acutely aware of her *déshabillé*. The thin silk nightgown did not hide much from his scrutiny.

"You ... are going to defend me against the gossipers, then? Take my side?"

"Yes, I am." He strolled toward her, until only a few inches of air separated their bodies. She could feel the overpowering virile heat of him, and her heartbeat raced alarmingly. There was nothing she could do to quiet it.

"I had planned a perfectly innocent and proper musicale," she whispered. "It's just that—"

"Shhh, don't mention this again. It was your initiation as a hostess, and a memorable one." He stressed the word initiation, and she had a powerful image that he expected other wifely duties to be initiated.

She thought she was going to faint under the pressure of the hot suggestion in his eyes. He touched her chin, tracing her jawline, slid his hand around her head to cup her neck.

"Come here, Allegra," he commanded.

She whimpered and took a tiny step toward him. He kissed her forehead. A sunbeam could not have burned her more. She gasped, her body rigid with apprehension. *Don't be such a ninny!* she admonished herself. *You are mightily taken with Wyndham. There's no denying it.* She stood on the tips of her toes and lifted her face toward his. Squeezing her eyes shut in fear, she waited for him to kiss her on the mouth. She heard the hiss of silk rubbing against silk as he lifted his other arm to pull her into his embrace. Waiting ... waiting, her heart lodged in her throat.

She was jerked out of the spell as he yelped and dropped his arms to his sides.

Allegra's eyes flew open and she stared aghast at the kitten climbing up Wyndham's dressing gown and sliding into the voluminous pocket.

"Blast and damnation! He stuck ten needles into my leg." He hauled the kitten up by the scruff of its neck and was about to toss it onto the bed. Beau, however, let out a drawn-out plaintive meow, and Wyndham ended up cradling the wiggling body against his chest. Soon Beau had squirmed up to his shoulder and sat there like a black sphinx surveying the world. His tail lay securely wrapped around Wyndham's neck.

"Oh, dear. I'm sorry, but Beau has no manners," Allegra said faintly.

"I suppose he's no better than the rest of the staff," Wyndham replied dryly and rubbed the kitten on the chest. "He, like so many others, was picked from the street."

Allegra sensed his exasperation and shrunk back against the bed. "I'm sorry if I've shown poor judgment in hiring the servants. I felt sorry for them, didn't want them to starve. I've never seen so many poor people as in London."

He gave his enigmatic smile, and she felt he'd closed a door to himself as the kitten climbed his leg. "A soft heart is both a curse and a blessing."

"Mayhap mostly a curse," she replied in an almost inaudible voice.

He sighed and lifted the cat to the bed. "A soft heart is vastly preferable than a hard one. I know." He strode to the door. "Good night, Allegra."

* * *

The next morning after breakfast, Allegra waited anxiously for the gossip to reach her ears. By midday she had heard nothing, and around noon Giles emerged from the blue guestroom and hunted her down in the walled garden behind the mansion.

"There you are, sis! You look blue-deviled. Did Wyndham give you a rare rakedown for the spectacle last night?"

"No, he couldn't have been more civil," Allegra said. She viewed her brother's good-natured sleepy face, eyes as blue as her own and hair the same chestnut color, his waving slightly more than hers.

"The entertaining was capital! I don't hold with musicales, make me fall asleep, but your gathering is something to remember for the rest of my life."

Allegra strolled along a brick path that meandered among borders of tulips and hyacinths, inhaling the aromatic scent of the flowers. Nervousness niggled at her, worrying about her reputation as a hostess, but most of all fretting about the mixed sensations that Wyndham inspired in her. She wished she could explain both the elation and the inexplicable pain in her heart.

"Capital to be in town, sis! Oxford is dull as ditch water." He walked past her on the path and reached a paved circle with two wrought-iron benches and a copper sundial surrounded by red tulips. He raked his hands through his hair as if agitated.

"I thought you enjoyed the merry company of your friends in Oxford. According to Stepfather, you don't do anything more useful than kick up wild larks."

He marched around the sundial and came to stand in front of her. The cheerful expression on his face had been replaced by anguish. "Dash it all, sis, but I'm sunk deep—in dun territory, that is. I need to get my dibs in tune."

Allegra added another worry to all her other ones. "Dear me! You're supposed to manage your allowance until end of term, Giles. Stepfather will be ever so vexed."

"I'm *badly* dipped, and that's a fact." He took a deep breath. "Three weeks ago I gambled the rest of my allowance and lost, sis."

Allegra moaned with exasperation. "Oh, no! How *could* you, Giles! Pinkney will be furious with you."

Giles's brow darkened, and he said stiffly, "Mr. Pinkney shall never know. Besides, the money was mine, left by father in trust. Pinkney has no say in the matter."

"He could pull you out of Oxford for this latest lark."

"I won't tell him about it, if you won't." Giles gave her a searching stare. "You won't tattle on me, will you?"

"Of course not!" she spat, pacing. "I'm not a tale bearer. But whatever will you do to come about?"

Giles took her hand and pulled her down on one of the benches. The sun warmed their faces and etched Giles features in stark relief. Every crease and twitch held despair.

"I have hopes you'll borrow me the necessary blunt, sis. After all, you're shackled to Wyndham, who has enough wealth to cover the paltry sum of my debt."

"I . . . I would dearly like to help you, but the thing is, I've already spent my quarterly allowance. In fact, I don't know how I'll get along until the end of the summer. Oh, Giles, I've been such a spendthrift!"

"Ask Wyndham for more funds."

Allegra cringed at the thought of having to display her wasteful ways to the earl. After all, he had instructed her to show a sense of economy. "What in the world shall we do? I don't have a feather to fly with."

Giles buried his head in his hands and braced his elbows on his knees. His body was a study of despair, and Allegra wished she hadn't spent so much money on gifts and fripperies. Embarrassed at her exorbitant spending in refurbishing the music room, she had used part of her allowance to pay for the costly brocade panels on the walls.

"I'm ruined. I'm dead," Giles said in sepulchral tones.

"Dead? Do you surround yourself with people who would rather see you dead than postpone the demand of payment?"

"Sis, I don't expect you to understand the code of a gentleman, but a gambling debt is expected to be settled immediately."

"You said you gambled away your allowance three weeks ago." Allegra rubbed her temples to subdue a spreading headache. "I don't quite understand."

Giles punched his knee with his clenched fist. "I've been such a muttonhead, sis." He turned his troubled eyes on Allegra, and she knew something much worse would be forthcoming. Giles always divulged his transgressions in stages of severity.

"I'm not sure I want to listen to you," she said, slowly pulling away.

"I have only you, sis!" he cried. "Who else could I turn to in my despair?"

He was right, of course. One didn't go to Mother for advice, nor did one approach Aunt Irene with monetary troubles. It simply wasn't done. "Very well, tell me the whole."

He took a deep breath and tore at his hair. "Well, I lost my last groat to Winky Alverton. Can't abide the fellow. A veritable popinjay, a scaly here-and-therian."

"Sounds like you," Allegra interrupted. "He could show some compassion."

"Allegra!" he cried in outrage. "If I hadn't paid up by the end of the next day, my reputation would have been in shreds. No one would take me seriously after that. Besides, Winky could have called me out. Pistols at dawn, y'know."

"Duels are illegal," Allegra said sternly. "You would not get embroiled in such an addled scheme."

"No . . . I paid my debt to Winky by borrowing from the moneylenders."

Allegra gasped, feeling faint. How many times had she heard Pinkney preach about the evils of the loan sharks? "How could you, Giles?"

"It's a dashed uncomfortable problem, sis. They are after me, y'know. The cents-per-cent dispatched a burly fellow after me to London to extract the first payment, and I ain't able to fork over the ready."

Despite his cant phrases, Allegra could decipher the horrifying news. "What will happen if he finds you?"

"I don't want to know! Suppose I'll hole up here until he goes away," Giles said gloomily. "That ham-fist can't very well knock on Wyndham's door and demand to see me. Dogwood will inform him that I ain't available."

"You'll have to pay the moneylenders. If you don't get out of debt immediately, they will only pull you down further. Pinkney told me about the evils of the exorbitant interest they demand." She searched her mind for a solution to the problem. "One of your friends could give you monetary support until you come about."

"They are as badly dipped as I am, but none has been so foolish as to—" He broke off and started pacing around the sun dial. " 'Zounds, how could I be so stupid—!"

Allegra found it hard to believe the depth of misery that people carried under the placid sunny surface of the spring day. Mutely she watched her brother move as if prodded by a demon.

"You'll have to help me," he begged.

chapter 11

"Giles, you'll have to approach Wyndham for a loan," Allegra said with finality.

Giles squirmed. "I don't know the man very well. Besides, he's not the kind of fellow who looks kindly upon deep gambling. He walks the straight and narrow. I don't want to appear a complete cad in his eyes." He pounced on Allegra's hand and squeezed it entreatingly. "You don't want me to look like a coxcomb, do you? Wyndham will never respect me if he gets wind of this."

Allegra chewed on her bottom lip. "I suppose there's some truth to that," she said, thinking of her husband's stern countenance. "But maybe he did the same things when he was younger. He might understand."

"Too principled a fellow, if you ask me," Giles blurted out. "Reduces me to nothing with those infernal sharp eyes of his."

"I surely prefer a principled gentleman to a reckless gambler," Allegra said tartly.

"He'll give you the blunt, sis. I know he will. He might lecture you for a minute or two but won't cut up rough. He'll come up with the dibs—ain't clutch-fisted like Pinkney."

"How much—" Allegra held her breath.

"Two thousand pounds."

"Two thousand . . . ?" Even though she'd never fainted, this would be the first time, Allegra thought as the world started revolving at a mad pace. Black edged her vision, and bile rose in her throat. She spread her fan and began fanning herself vigorously. Searching for something to say, she opened her mouth, but no words emerged.

Giles pale face hovered anxiously above her. "Don't fly into a pet, sis. Fact is fact, and there ain't much I can do to lower the sum owed. Truth is, it rises steeply every day."

"You'll have to pay off the whole amount, or you'll never get away from the cents-per-cent," Allegra croaked as she regained her speech. The world slowed, and she realized she wouldn't swoon after all.

"I know. That's why it's important that you approach the earl as soon as may be." Giles pulled her to her feet. "There ain't no time like the present."

There was no other way than to confide in Wyndham and seek his advice. He would surely despise her when he discovered that she'd spent all of her allowance. Not that it would have covered Giles's debt . . . far from it. But—

After giving her brother a glare, she went into the house on wooden legs. It took a minute for her eyes to adjust to the twilight inside, and she waited, thinking of ways to broach the subject with her husband.

She found Knocky in the hallway. His face held a glum expression. "What's the matter, Knocky?" Allegra asked, for a moment forgetting Giles's problem.

"The Master give me a ribbin' fer last night. Ye've niver 'eard anythin' like it. Me ears are still smartin' sumthin' arful."

She threw a glance toward the door, noticing that Francis and Xerxes were at their posts, their expressions as glum as Knocky's. "I daresay the earl was in a rare taking."

"Not 'e, me lady. 'E's cool as ye please, but 'is wrath is *cold*. It gave me th' shivers, an' no mistake."

"You well deserved it. His Lordship could have kicked you out without a groat in your pocket." The thought of money turned her attention back to her problem. "Is His Lordship in the library?"

"Yes, melady." Knocky walked sedately, not skipped, in front of her to the door that led to the lion's lair. Her legs trembled so much she could barely walk. With difficulty she dismissed the impulse to run away and hide in her bedroom. The faster she tackled the problem, the sooner it would be solved. No need to prolong the pain—

"By the way, Knocky, where did you learn to play the pianoforte?"

"Played the organ at Cripplegate Church I did, and sang, too. The curate taught me," Knocky said importantly.

Knocky opened the door and stood aside. She swallowed nervously. "Wyndham? Can you spare a minute of your time?" she asked, her voice quivering disgustingly.

He rose from the chair behind the desk and smiled in welcome. "Certainly. I'm only working on the boring accounts. Your company would not be amiss."

Allegra entered and the door closed behind her with an ominous click. She was inside the prison cell, and there was no way out.

"A lovely morning," she said, just to open the conversation.

He came toward her, that unsettling smile on his face. He kissed her cheek, the fragrance of his soap touching her nostrils. His hand was warm around hers, and she gripped it as if were a rock in a stormy sea.

"This is a pleasant surprise," he said. "You haven't visited me in this room before."

How true. Dazed, Allegra viewed the book-lined walls and the comfortable leather chairs by the fireplace. The old Oriental carpet lent a cozy air to the room, as did the smell of brandy and old books.

"There always has to be a first time," Allegra said.

"I had the feeling you were reluctant to pay me a visit here."

Allegra looked away. "I didn't want to intrude."

"Nonsense! You're not an intruder in my life, rather a longed-for diversion." He smiled, and Allegra wished she could throw her arms around him and hug him.

He looked elegant in buff pantaloons and a double-breasted frock coat. Oglesby had barbered the earl's hair, and his chin was clean shaven. All in all, he made a very attractive picture, and Allegra's heart jumped into her throat. Her love for him threatened to rise up and choke her. Her mission was impossible! She couldn't stand the thought of seeing his pleasure replaced by disgust as she revealed her problem.

"Is there something you need to speak to me about?" he asked smoothly.

She only looked to the floor, unable to put her problem into words—or Giles's problem really, but she was reluctant to reveal her brother's spendthrift ways to Wyndham.

He went back to the desk and waited for her to sit down on the opposite chair before resuming his seat. "Allegra, do you need to talk about the refurbishing projects? I'm going through the bills right now, thinking them rather steep. Yet, I realize the rooms desperately need the work done."

Allegra flinched. "Are you implying that I'm spending too much?"

He smiled pleasantly. "No, not at all. I simply didn't understand the extent of the repairs needed. Our expenses might have to be scrutinized more closely. Not that I begrudge a single penny spent on the house, mind you, but I don't like the workmen to take advantage of your tender age and inspire you to buy the most expensive, and mayhap not the best quality, goods."

Wallowing in a sea of guilt, Allegra glanced everywhere but at her husband. How could she ask for an advance on her allowance? "I understand. I'll try to be more careful in the future."

His mentioning of her tender age might have inspired her anger, but the earl was right, wasn't he? She was a miss right out of the schoolroom and must be treated as such. His face held the hint of a patient, indulgent smile. That expression sank her spirits to the deepest chasm of despair. He would never see her in any other light than a younger sister, a hoydenish one.

"I pray you slept well, my dear? After all, it was rather an upheaval last night."

Allegra perched on the edge of her seat, mauling a pleat of her mint-green muslin gown between her fingers. "I slept the sleep of the innocent," she lied.

"I heard Giles's voice in the garden. Does he have to return to Oxford instantly?"

"No ... he has some time in London. I'm excessively glad to see him, but—" Allegra's mouth clamped shut as she viewed Wyndham across the desk. How could she broach the subject of Giles's debts? Now was the perfect moment, but deep shame burned in her heart, and she couldn't find the courage to bring up her brother's disgrace—and her own.

"But? Why do I detect a note of apprehension in your voice?"

Allegra drew a deep breath. "My lord! Ian, I ... have sadly squandered my allowance. All of it." She cringed as she waited for his icy censure, but his lips tilted in a lopsided grin.

"I suppose you gave away too many alms and bought too many snuffboxes," he said with a sigh of resignation. "Your generosity is highly commendable, Allegra, but you must learn to keep order to your finances."

She lowered her gaze, humiliation burning in her cheeks.

"Will a hundred pounds see you through?"

She wanted to blurt out *two thousand*, but the amount was too ridiculously high to even mention. In her eyes a hundred pounds was a small fortune, and she couldn't possibly ask for more. A vivid image of a cent-per-cent in a voluminous black cloak and wearing a sinister sneer confronting Giles in some dark alley made her almost cry.

"I can see that you are very upset," Wyndham went on, kindly. "No need to suffer such remorse, my dear."

"Thank you, Ian. You're very understanding, I think."

"Well, since we're in such harmony with each other, I see this as the perfect moment to present you with another gift." He went to a cabinet and unlocked a drawer. After pulling out a large flat case, he turned to Allegra with an expectant smile.

She waited tensely for him to reveal his surprise.

"I don't know when it would be a good time to give you this, Allegra, so I do it now. It belonged to my mother, and before that to every Countess of Wyndham for the last three hundred years." He stood before her and opened the lid. The fiery sparkle of large diamonds and small made her gasp in surprise.

"The Wyndham Diamonds. I had them cleaned and set in gold filigree. The old setting seemed too pompous, fit only for a dowager."

Allegra touched the circle of large rose-cut jewels that tapered off in size toward the clasp. "Surely they are too grand for me." Daunted, she could only stare at the fortune in diamonds. Having grown up at a small country estate, she had rather simple tastes. The sapphire necklace, the bracelet that Wyndham had given her, a slender gold chain with a opal pendant, and her gold locket with the four-leaf clover composed her jewelry collection.

"You don't have to wear them very often if you don't wish. But for grand occasions, they are just the perfect accessory, don't you agree?"

"I suppose," Allegra said dubiously but accepted the leather case. She stared at the diamonds until they swirled into a mass of shooting sparks and blue flashes. They simply took her breath away.

His long fingers pulled the necklace from its bed of black velvet. "You must try them on."

Allegra had no such desire, but she obeyed, rising to stand in front of him as he clasped the cold stones around her neck. Thank goodness she had a long neck that could show off such a heavy necklace, she thought.

Wyndham's warm breath caressed her nape, and she took a startled step forward.

He chuckled derisively. "Skittish, by God. I wasn't about to take a bite out of your neck."

"I ... I didn't fear that," she said, fingering the necklace.

"What did you fear?" he asked in a silky voice and took a step closer to her.

"Nothing—nothing at all, my lord—Ian."

"Mayhap you pictured something utterly more sinister than a bite?" He stood so close she could study the laugh lines bracketing his mouth in great intimacy. She started in surprise as he suddenly pulled her into a hard embrace. "A kiss, not on your neck, but on your lips. Not that I wasn't tempted to taste your vulnerable neck, sweet wife."

"Ian—" she uttered in fainting tones.

Without ado, he caught her trembling lips with his in an open-mouthed kiss that robbed her of all her senses. She'd never been more shocked, yet something awakened in the pit of her stomach, a fiery warmth that spiraled downward and pooled into her loins. No feeling like it had ever invaded her body.

She pushed weakly against his hard chest as his tongue plundered the silky insides of her mouth. His grip tightened as if he were tired of her struggle. The kiss deepened, forcing a whirlwind of feverish sensation through her until she could stand no longer. Without his support, she would have crumpled onto the carpet.

When he finally lifted his face away from hers, she could barely find the strength to breathe. His gaze had darkened, fixed upon her lips with an expression of incredulity and—awe? Unsure of how to react, she gently pulled away. He jerked aside as if slapped, and she wondered what had caused his abrupt reaction. A flush had crept into his lean cheeks. Could he be embarrassed? she wondered, suddenly amused.

His eyes flashed, and he cleared his throat. "The diamonds look lovely, but that gown does nothing to set them off."

Allegra remembered that she was wearing a demure high-necked muslin gown. A deep décolletage, a rounded bosom would show off the diamonds, and she couldn't brag about overly prominent endowments. Like a streak of heat, his gaze swept over her from head to toe.

"Wear them sometimes," he said in a way of dismissing her.

"Yes, Ian. Thank you." She stumbled on a crease in the carpet as she hurried toward the door. Making an undignified exit, she cursed herself for her clumsiness.

Giles was hovering outside in the hallway, ostentatiously studying the dull portraits of Wyndham forebears. When had Giles cultivated an interest in art? Never. He easily tore himself away from his deep study and accosted Allegra.

He asked in a low urgent voice, "What did Wyndham say? Did he give you the money?"

Allegra remembered her failure to bring up the subject. It was now too late. "He . . . well, I *could not* ask him for such an enormous sum of money, Giles!" she said in a loud whisper and glanced at the motionless footmen by the door. "Let's go into the blue parlor."

She dragged her brother by the arm into the nearby salon that had received its name by the predominant blue color of the decor. It gave an impression of cool elegance, striking a chord with the cold apprehension in Allegra's chest. She felt a need to examine her exciting encounter with Wyndham, but Giles's problem took precedent.

"Whatever shall I do?" Giles moaned and tore at his chestnut curls. "I'll be ruined!"

"You *are* already ruined, Giles," Allegra pointed out with some asperity. "Come, we must sit down and try to form a plan to rescue you from the moneylenders."

"Couldn't you tell Wyndham you need the funds to clean the portraits in the foyer or something?"

"Then I would have to show him the results. Besides, he was somewhat taken aback by the high amount I spent on the music room. He'll keep an eye on the bills, I know he will."

"He's a worse skinflint than Mr. Pinkney," Giles burst out.

"No, he's not! Wyndham is only careful; he's not tightfisted." Allegra marveled at her desire to defend her husband. When had he ever needed a champion? If he did, it wouldn't be her support he sought, surely?

Giles stared hard at her, a wild expression in his eyes. "There's only one thing for it, sis. You'll have to pawn something that can be retrieved later." He glanced pointedly at the diamonds still hanging around her neck.

She gasped. "You don't mean the Wyndham Diamonds? They are worth a grand fortune. Wyndham gave me these just now."

"Would nicely cover the debt. We would only borrow the round sum of two thousand pounds against the necklace."

Allegra looked at him in shock. "From whom?"

He squirmed in the sofa beside her and wrought more havoc to his hair. "I have *connections*. Leave it all to me."

"If I do, I'm not likely to ever see the diamonds again," she said darkly. "No ... you'll have to lay the whole before me, and then we'll see."

He colored and squirmed some more. "Well, there's a certain lady I visit. She's a wealthy woman in her own right, runs a house—" He stopped abruptly and threw a wild glance at Allegra.

"House? What kind of house? A hotel?"

"Ahh, yes ... a respectable hotel. She's been a particular friend of mine these last two years, and she would help me out, I'm sure."

Allegra narrowed her eyes as suspicion flowed through her veins. "Why wouldn't she aid you from the start? Why didn't you turn to her directly?"

"She—well—she would need a security deposit on a loan, of course. Business is business." His eyes coveted the diamond necklace. "She would take good care of the gems while I raise the blunt to pay her back and retrieve the necklace."

"And how, pray tell, would you go about that?" Allegra had a sinking feeling in her stomach and knew she didn't want to hear his vague reply.

"Oh ... I shall come about. Not to worry. Like you, I was blessed with uncommon luck from the outset."

"Luck does not necessarily bring you happiness, or that what you desire," she said sagely.

He gave her an incredulous glance. "You must admit that luck brought you to the position you're in today! Wyndham would not have looked twice at you—begging your pardon, sis—if it hadn't been for that wild notion of yours to run away from home."

"Maybe, but I would have preferred happiness before luck," she said, thinking about the difficulty in being the Countess of Wyndham. "I wasn't exactly *groomed* for this position in society."

"You'll get used to your role, and that's all there is to it." Giles got up and started pacing.

Allegra watched him and hoped he would learn something from this dire situation, but she doubted it. "I suppose Wyndham would not miss the diamonds for a couple of weeks, if that is as long as your business will take. I cannot leave them out of the house for an interminable time."

Giles face lit up. "You're an angel! I knew I could count on you to help me out of this pickle, sis. I shan't forget your support."

And so it was decided. Allegra kept the diamonds around her neck for the span of fifteen minutes, then they disappeared into Giles's pocket, and she prayed she would see them again soon. She wouldn't be able to sleep a wink until they were back under the Wyndham roof and locked away.

chapter 12

Giles returned on the following day bearing news that the necklace was in the capable hands of a Mrs. Sally Spinks, a decisive lady of many—ahem—talents, he informed Allegra.

"Did you pay off the moneylender?" she asked anxiously.

"I did, late last night. No more to worry about, sis. As long as it'll take to get the funds, I'll remain as snug as a pea in the pod at the card tables at Brook's. I will surely win—"

Allegra clapped her hands to her ears to close out the wild, confident words. Nothing good was bound to come out of his gambling. "I don't want to hear about it! Furthermore, I will not accept another account that you've lost your shirt at the cardtables. I will not help you out of another financial scrape!"

"No need to take on so, sis."

"I hope you learned a lesson from this." Her hands clamped on her hips, she gave him an ominous scowl. "If it weren't for my help, you would be in the dark pits of *despair* by now."

"You're right. I've learned the errors of my ways. I

won't ever be so reckless again." Giles gave her a nervous smile and made himself scarce.

Allegra feared her efforts at instilling sense had been for naught. A leopard didn't change his spots, did he? She touched her locket, wondering if a four-leaf clover truly brought the luck it was famed for.

One week later Wyndham was getting ready for the Duchess of Newberry's ball. He struggled with the intricate knot of his neckcloth, and behind him, Oglesby was brushing his best tailcoat of charcoal satin. The white silk stockings made his feet damp, and he abhorred the knee-breeches that always reduced him to feeling like a veritable popinjay.

Not that he had any great desire to attend the ball, but he'd promised to escort Allegra, and he was loath to break his promise. Especially to his wife, whom he'd come to care for more than he thought possible. She displayed such thoughtfulness and kindness it was hard not to care. Besides, the gloomy mansion had truly taken on a cheerful welcoming air. Allegra had a good rapport with the servants, who showed their appreciation by making the mansion shine with much scrubbing and polish. Delicious aromas from the kitchen found their way along the stately walls. They all appeared to be happy, going about their chores with zest—all except Dogwood, who walked about with a perpetually pained expression, due to Knocky's cheeky presence. The positive change would be credited to his shy young bride. Wyndham chuckled to himself. Honey attracted more bees than vinegar, and no one had a sweeter disposition than Allegra.

That was it; with goodness she brought life to his house and soothed the ache in his heart. Come to think of it, his thoughts had not lingered on Justine overly much this last week. The realization excited him, and new life, like a brisk spring breeze, raced through his veins.

"Oglesby, this collar is very good. Just the right amount of starch. I thought I was forever doomed to collars that would chafe my skin raw."

Oglesby sighed as if hard put upon. "I don't know how many times I cautioned the laundress about the starch, but to no avail."

Wyndham raised his eyebrows and finished brushing his hair in the mirror. "Then what did you do to convince her to change her ways?"

"It wasn't me, my lord. Her Ladyship had a word with the staff when she noticed your problem with the starch."

Wyndham let out a bark of laughter. "She is a regular little housekeeper, isn't she?"

"Oh, no, my lord, a true chatelaine. She knows how to make everyone comfortable, including the staff."

The earl set down his brush and the valet eased the tight coat over Wyndham's shoulders. "I daresay she's a trifle young to have learned such skills so rapidly, Oglesby."

"Some ladies have a natural talent for it, my lord."

"She's making this sad pile into a home, Oglesby. I take it the servants have no complaints?"

Oglesby's serious face gave the hint of a smile. "Oh, no, my lord. The others like the new mistress very much, as do I."

Warmed by those words, the earl made sure his white waistcoat of watered silk did not show any creases. He arranged two gold fobs across the front to brighten the starkness of his attire. Then he went downstairs to await his wife's appearance.

In the library he poured himself a glass of brandy from a crystal decanter. He couldn't remember a day when he'd felt more at peace, certainly not since Justine jilted him. Narrowing his eyes to ward off the familiar stab of pain, he was relieved to notice that it didn't accost him. Justine ... she'd turned waspish lately, and her eyes held a hectic expression as she swirled from one entertainment to the next. She fluttered like a moth, singeing her wings on pleasures too bright. He sensed that his erstwhile fiancée was unhappy, and he suspected that she suffered from the same malady as he did, a broken heart. He should be delighted that she suffered, but he couldn't find anything but compassion in his heart.

His thought broke off abruptly as Xerxes opened the door for Allegra. She swept in, wearing a pearl-encrusted cream ball gown that moved seductively around her ankles as she approached him with a smile. Her hair was upswept into a crown of curls, pearly combs glinting, and she wore a chain with an opal pendant around her regal neck. The small gold locket was as usual pinned unobtrusively to her bodice. Her innocent beauty took his breath away. Surely, she seemed years older than at their wedding day? Impossible. Only weeks had passed since that event.

"You're a vision of loveliness," he said truthfully and kissed her hand. "Would you like a glass of wine before we leave?"

"Yes ... that would be good. I can use some to steady my nerves."

He poured sherry into a crystal glass and handed it to her. "Are you worried about the ball?"

"The Duchess is a very grand person, isn't she? Almost as grand as the Queen."

"A crusty old lady, but she's entertaining. Fearless horsewoman. Used to ride a hunter as well as any man in her heyday."

"She will disapprove of me," Allegra said, sipping nervously on the wine.

"Nonsense! The whole of London is still talking about

the musicale. You made an instant success with your unusual entertainment."

Allegra made a moue. "Yes, I now wear epithets as the Original, or Eccentric Lady Wyndham."

His lips raised in a smile. "I rather like the 'Dashing' young Lady Wyndham."

Allegra smiled ruefully. "Is that what they say at the clubs?"

He nodded and raised his glass. His eyes twinkled wickedly. "I'm proud."

"I'm certainly grateful that you're not crusty, Ian. I thought—well, that you were rather high in the instep, at first," she blurted out.

"I appreciate your frankness," he said dryly. "But I pride myself on being in possession of a slight sense of humor. I daresay that the musicale and the following *picnic* touched that insignificant part of my personality."

"I'd say you have rather a great sense for the ridiculous." She smiled coquettishly at him, and the earl blinked hard. His child bride was rapidly turning into a seductive woman.

"I'm pleased that you appreciate my insignificant sterling qualities," he murmured, fighting a wild urge to sweep her into his arms.

"You underestimate yourself, my lord. Your qualities are golden."

"And you are a diamond of the first water." He took a step toward her.

"My heart is sinking like a stone—a plain pebble, that is," she whispered as a shadow of apprehension moved across her face.

"Are you afraid of me? Is that what you're trying to tell me?" he asked in a choked voice. God, a rage of emotions was threatening to overcome him.

"No . . . yes, perhaps a little."

"No need to be." He touched a silky wayward curl. "That sinking feeling can be quite pleasurable if you but let it."

"Pinkney would call such emotion unseemly in a young lady."

He chuckled. "Mr. Pinckney is forever out of your way, Allegra. What does he know about sinking feelings?"

Allegra giggled. "He does instantly know about the *sinking* of the value of his stocks."

"That is as far as his heart will ever sink—to wealth," Wyndham said. "He knows naught of more nobler feelings."

"Do you?" Allegra whispered.

She seemed to be holding her breath, her eyes fixed on his like two blazing sapphires. *Yes!* he wanted to shout. *I've known the heights of euphoria, and the deepest depths of despair.* He didn't say any of those words, however, and turned aside slowly. He was aware of a growing happiness inside. He wanted to be sure that Allegra was the source of that sensation before he said something to her he might regret later.

"I hope so," he said noncommittally. He moved smoothly to his desk and pulled out a drawer. "I have something for you that I saved for this occasion." He looked at her, seeing the closing of her face as if she were a rose that had opened up to the sun of his adoration, then closed as darkness fell. Could it be that his wife had fallen in love with him? The question struck him like a hard blow, and he staggered under its implication.

Allegra studied his bemused face, wishing she could read the thoughts going through his mind. Her heart raced furiously, and she abhorred herself for bringing up a question that would only remind him of his pain. Of course he'd experienced nobler feelings. *Justine.* He'd been in love with her, and probably still was. He'd known happiness as well as pain, and Allegra had familiarized herself with that pain, because it echoed in her own heart. As long as Justine stood between them, they would remain polite strangers.

"Here, it's only a trifle."

Allegra received a fan, a carved ivory brisé fan, the pattern so intricate and delicate the bone seemed as translucent as thin paper. She gasped with pleasure. "It's exquisite." She studied his face. "Why? It is not my birthday."

"No, but you have made my life so much easier, and this is my way of showing my appreciation. It's only a worthless trinket."

"Thank you."

"I hope you shall use it tonight." He stood so close, she could feel the heat of him. Her heart jumped into her throat, and she wondered if her legs would support her much longer. Especially as he was giving her that lazy grin accompanied by a wealth of suggestion.

He touched the gold locket lightly. "What do you hide here? A miniature of your childhood sweetheart?"

Heat moved up her throat and into her face. "Not at all! It used to be my paternal grandmother's, a wedding gift, I believe. I keep a four-leaf clover in it—for luck."

"Ahh, my wife is superstitious!"

"Giles says I have uncommon good luck."

He stared at her, evidently pondering her words. "Mayhap he's right, but then again, Giles is bound to exaggerate. Why should some people have more luck than others?"

Allegra smiled in deviltry. "Mayhap some find four-leaf clovers to aid them and most don't."

"Hmm, I'm surprised your brother has not stolen it from you to enhance his luck at the gambling tables. He's been ensconced at Brook's for the last sennight, and I fear he'll come away badly dipped."

Allegra clasped her new fan so hard she thought she would break it. All her suppressed fear welled up inside her. What if Giles didn't manage to raise the funds to get the Wyndham Diamonds back from Mrs. Spinks? The thought could not be borne.

"He always was involved in wild schemes, and I fear his being away at Oxford has not helped. He didn't go back to university like planned."

"Would you like me to have a word with him?"

Allegra blanched. "No! That will not be necessary. Giles must find a way to fend for himself, learn responsibility. He always was a shocking wastrel." And the trait travels perhaps in the family, she thought, remembering her own empty purse. "He'll go back to Oxford after our ball here. The end of next week." Allegra cringed as she realized she would have to live with nerve-racking uncertainty about the necklace another week.

"Very well. Let's take ourselves to Lady Newberry's ball. I daresay it'll be a crushing bore."

Allegra set her new fan to work. "Well, a 'crush' is the proof of success, you know."

"You have learned a lot since you came to London, wife," Wyndham said with a chuckle. "You will do very well, indeed."

Allegra lapped up the praise, pleasure filling her whole body. If anything, she would certainly enjoy the crush—even if Justine was there and danced with Wyndham.

chapter 13

All the windows of Newberry House on Piccadilly blazed with candles and oil lamps. A long row of carriages slowly paraded past the front steps, letting off guests in lustrous seductive satins, rainbow-hued silks, velvets, and jewels of all shapes and sizes. Diamonds glittered and blazed with white fire, rubies glowed, and sapphires shot cool mystical sparks. Allegra had never seen such a fortune in gems assembled in one place.

Proud of her escort, she entered on Wyndham's arm and felt a surge of pleasure as the butler barked their names, "The Earl and Countess of Wyndham."

They swept inside, and Allegra found that she did not blush as the Duchess of Newberry, her leathery throat encased in a set of enormous diamonds, shook Allegra's fingertips. Her old blue eyes glinted mischievously. "How good to see you, Lady Wyndham. The town is talking about you as the most dashing hostess of the season."

Now Allegra blushed, but she could not detect any frigid hauteur in the other woman's expression. "I do hope you can attend our ball next week, Your Grace. I promise there won't be any picnics on the floor or servants singing in the hallway."

"Why not? We need some refreshing entertainment, my dear!"

Thus praised, Allegra greeted the rest of the family, then hooked onto Wyndham's arm as he escorted her toward the ballroom upstairs. She met Aunt Irene and Lydia Sinclair. Giles had been invited, but there was no sign of him—thank God. Anyway, he would probably arrive late.

"May I have the first dance?" Wyndham inquired, and Allegra blushed with pleasure. They went with other couples to form a minuet, and the earl didn't take his eyes off her face as they performed the intricate steps. Allegra had never been more aware of him, or herself. Her blood sang, her heart fluttered like a trapped butterfly in her chest, and a curiously warm weakness invaded her stomach. Surely, he was the most handsome gentleman in the room.

To her surprise, his half smile stiffened, and his set face paled as he moved in the dance. She noticed the reason— Justine Bryerly on her right. Justine looked lovely in a gown of eggshell-white lace, a simple strand of pearls around her slim throat. Her lovely face held an expression of tragic despair.

The pleasure of the dance was ruined by Justine's appearance. Yet she would have been invited, no reason to think otherwise. Allegra wished she could hate her old friend, but she found only disgust for herself, for hoping against hope that Wyndham was falling in love with her. Hoping that he'd forgotten his ill-fated attraction to Justine.

When the dance was over, Wyndham led her off the floor. "If you excuse me, Allegra, I'll have a chat with a friend of mine."

Who? Allegra wanted to ask, but held her tongue. She only nodded stiffly. "You're not tied to my apron strings, you know."

"Thank you," he said with a wry smile.

Filled with longing, she watched his broad back as he strolled among the guests. She didn't wait to see who had caught his attention. Aunt Irene stepped forward, putting her arm through Allegra's. "Let's go out onto the terrace. It's stifling in here. These squeezes put me out of temper."

"Yes, it is shockingly hot tonight."

A soft breeze cooled their faces outside, and Allegra inhaled deeply, trying to wipe out the memory of Wyndham's stricken face as he gazed at Justine.

"You seem heavy-hearted," Aunt Irene said. "Is there a problem?"

"No . . . well, yes. I don't know. Why ask?" She leaned into her aunt's shoulder and let the tears burning the back of her eyes sweep forward. "I do declare 'tis difficult to be married." She gulped down a sob, quickly brushing away the wetness from her eyes.

Aunt Irene patted her niece's back. "I do believe you have grown up, sweet Allegra. It's a painful procedure. I know I shouldn't pry, but are you—happy—with Wyndham?"

Allegra nodded her head vigorously. "He's a good, honorable gentleman."

"A trifle stiff, perhaps?"

"No, not at all!" Allegra blurted out. "He has a lively sense of humor and is quite talkative. Discusses all manner of subjects with me—as he would with his friends."

Aunt Irene said nothing in response.

"I like to think that he considers me his friend," Allegra whispered and took another swipe at her eyes.

"I think you would like him to consider you more than that," Aunt Irene said practically.

"Mayhap." Allegra could not take the pain of having her feelings analyzed. She pulled away from her aunt's comforting arms and walked along the terrace alone. Yearning for a moment to collect herself, she was grateful that Irene had not followed her. She ought not be out here skulking in the shadows. Who knows what guests she might come across? The terrace was a good trysting place for lovers.

Wyndham did not see his wife anywhere on the dance floor and decided to seek refuge in the gambling room set aside for the pleasure of the gentlemen guests. By the door, he ran into Percy Harcombe.

"Where is fair Allegra?" Percy asked immediately.

"Chatting with her cronies, no doubt," the earl said. "I left her by the dance floor." He studied his cousin, resplendent in a black coat and gold-embroidered waistcoat.

"I would not leave the side of such beauty," Percy said with a deep sigh of feeling.

"I'm sure you'll find her if you look. She'll be pleased to see you, I'm sure," the earl said with a faint smile.

Percy threw up his hands. "How unfeeling you are! Are you not the tiniest bit jealous, Wyndham?"

The earl grinned. "Of you, coz? Not in the slightest."

"Cold-hearted snob," Percy said with a sniff.

"How about a hand of whist? I can always use some coins in my rapidly shrinking coffers."

Percy followed with alacrity. " 'Tis I who shall replenish my funds. I might give the winnings to your poor wife."

Wyndham whipped his head around. "Why would you do that?"

"Well . . ." Percy drew out the word and gave his cousin an intent stare. "Last time—was it yesterday?—I took Allegra to the cloth merchants, and she was reluctant to choose anything. When I prodded for an explanation to her sudden tightfisted behavior, she claimed that she would have to watch her purse."

Wyndham barked a laugh. "The devil she did!"

Percy nodded. "Are you keeping her on stringent rations, coz?"

"Of course not! I only asked her to practice economy. Besides, I'm sure the merchants take advantage of her youth, her inexperience."

"That is mighty unfair, Wyndham! Would I let the merchants fleece her if I'm present?"

Wyndham patted Percy's shoulder. "No, I don't believe that for a moment."

"You're a nodcock, Wyndham."

"I've heard worse." The earl scratched his cheek in thought. "Do you say she seemed dipped or just reluctant to tally up the bills."

"She doesn't have many farthings to tally, Ian. Dipped, I'd say. She always gives the beggars a few coins during our outings, but she has given nothing lately. I didn't realize you'd turned into a nip-farthing in your old age."

"I gave her—" Wyndham stared into space, barely aware of Giles Temple greeting him with a hearty slap on the back.

"A dreadful bore, ain't it?" Giles said. "Thank God I escaped in here before the duchess dragooned me into dancing with the antidotes along the walls."

"That would have been a great sacrifice," Percy said dryly. "Are you up to losing some goldfinches, young fellow?"

Giles smiled broadly and rubbed his hands. "That's why I'm here. Not to lose, but to *win*. I feel luck is on my side tonight. Allegra's four-leaf clover would positively *glow* if it were anywhere near me."

Wyndham turned abruptly on his heel. "If you'll excuse me, gentlemen. I have a score to settle."

Wyndham heard Giles's shocked outcry, but he forged a path among the guests, all the while scanning for his wife. Could it be she had monetary problems and didn't dare to approach him? Suddenly it had become imperative that he find her so that he could reassure himself that she wasn't too apprehensive to confide her troubles in him. He had been so sure that she'd overcome her wariness—except in matters of a more intimate nature. They had arrived at friendship, so why wouldn't she confide her difficulties? Had their marriage so wobbly a foundation on which to stand? The suspicion shattered him. If he lost her confidence ... Had he ever gained it? If not, all the ground he'd established with her was for naught.

He looked at the dance floor but didn't see her. Evidently she had left the ballroom. He didn't blame her; the room was hot as hell.

Where the deuce was she hiding? He sprinted downstairs and looked into the salons. One of them, a small chamber by the door, held all the wraps and hats that the guests had discarded. There, on a sofa, in the gloom lit only by one candle, sat a woman. He rushed in.

"Allegra? Is that you?"

The lady raised her drooping head, and he looked into Justine's tragic eyes. "Justine?" His voice abandoned him. Torn between a desire to go in search of Allegra and the urge to comfort his erstwhile fiancée, he stepped forward. "What's the matter? You look as pale as a ghost."

Gingerly, feeling a stab of guilt for sitting down next to an unwed lady in a darkened room, he joined her. He took her cold hand into his and patted it. "Tell me what's wrong."

"Lewington left ten minutes ago, said he never wanted to see me again," she explained in a toneless voice.

"Well, good riddance! Why do you wear your heart upon your sleeve? That fellow isn't worth your adoration. He's a cold fish of a man who uses everyone who comes across his path."

"That's a gross exaggeration," she scoffed. "You're only jealous because I gave my heart to him."

"That might be true. I know we've always been frank with each other, Justine, but that tone of disdain won't do. You've trampled on my heart enough."

She looked at him, her pained eyes shimmering with tears. "I was monstrously unfair to you, Wyndham, but you will thank me in the end for what I did. We would not have suited, would always have been at loggerheads. I have no patience for things domestic, and you're a man who thrives on comfort around you, a wife who adores you and rushes to please you."

Just the kind of wife I have, Wyndham thought. "The heart does not take into consideration such trivial details when it decides to give itself."

"You are a better person for the pain you've felt—more humble," Justine went on inexorably, "as I will be once I forget Lewington. If ever."

"Of course you'll get over that scoundrel," Wyndham said and stood. Impatience was eating at him, and he longed to be gone from the room.

"Listen to yourself," she muttered scathingly.

He did, and realized that his flippant remark was true. In his case. He had gotten over his love, or call it infatuation, for Justine, and could with certainty give the advice that she would get over Lewington. "There is always another day—when the pain will be less."

She said, "Then there will come a day, when it is wholly gone. Is that what you were about to say, Wyndham?" She looked at him knowingly, and he nodded imperceptibly.

"Yes."

She held out her hand and raised her chin. "Goodbye, Wyndham. May I call you friend?"

"Of course!" With a rueful laugh, he pulled her to her

feet. "You'll soon find the man who will truly love you. Come along. I'll find your mother, and she shall take you home."

He opened the door and let her out ahead of him. He could not recall a time when his heart had felt lighter.

Allegra watched them from the top of the stairs, an icy fear gripping her. Wyndham bore an expression of happiness, and she wondered what had transpired between him and Justine. Allegra had noted Lewington's absence and Justine's sagging shoulders. Did it mean that Justine tried to seek happiness in Wyndham's arms if Lewington had abandoned her?

Allegra didn't really want to know the answer. Tearing away her gaze from the couple, she melted into the crowd of guests. She would stay away from Wyndham until it was time to go home.

At midnight she had supper with Percy and Giles. There was no sign of Wyndham until the very end of the midnight hour. He looked preoccupied, only gave her the vaguest of smiles, and Allegra's heart plummeted. She feared his mind was filled with visions of the lovely Justine, and his heart overflowing with yearning.

There was, however, no sign of Justine.

At two o'clock, Allegra pleaded a headache and asked Wyndham to take her home.

"Certainly, my dear. It has been a tiring night." He arranged with a footman to fetch her shawl, then made a path among the guests to their hosts. Allegra was grateful for his control of the situation. She took her farewells, and complimented the duchess on her splendid gathering.

Feeling less than splendid, she let Wyndham lead her out to the carriage. Sometimes it was just too hard to maintain her optimism and good will.

The coachman closed the door to the coach and tooled

the equipage around a line of carriages to reach the street. The night had a distinct chill as if reminding the people of London that, not too long ago, winter had held the city in its formidable grip.

Allegra shuddered as she sank back against the silk squabs.

"Are you cold?" Without waiting for an answer, Wyndham took off his elegant coat and spread it around her shoulders. "That should warm you."

"But now you'll be cold," Allegra said.

He laughed, a carefree sound that warmed her more than the coat. "Don't worry about me. I'm rather warm-blooded." His voice held a hint of suggestion, and Allegra's heart jumped alarmingly.

"You sound . . . happy, Wyndham," she said cautiously. "Did something of interest happen at the ball?"

"You could say that," he replied cryptically. "I discovered something about myself, and something about you."

Remembering the Wyndham Diamonds, Allegra swallowed in apprehension. "Did you learn that I am a mediocre dancer? Well, my sense of rhythm is not what it ought to be." Her effort to lighten up the tense atmosphere fell flat.

"I haven't yet held you in my arms in the waltz, so I can't say if you'll maul my feet or not." He nudged her chin. "I suspect you won't."

He placed his arm casually around her shoulder and pulled her closer. The heat of his body entered hers, giving comfort. "I need to speak with you about something that disturbs me, Allegra."

She held her breath, waiting for a blistering rakedown for some ill she could not remember. Unless he'd found out about the Wyndham Diamonds. "I'm innocent," she said flippantly, but the words lay uneasy on her tongue.

"I found out by chance, from Percy, that you have pockets to let. Is that true?"

Allegra shrank away from him. "Why would Percy think that? We've been spending hours in the warehouses choosing and buying material for the house."

"Percy claims you would not buy anything, constantly worrying about the cost. And you don't show charity to the beggars," he went on inexorably.

"Well, I can't support them on a handful of coppers," she snapped.

Wyndham pondered her words in silence, and she heard him heave a deep sigh. "I wish you would confide your problems in me. I'm not the ogre you believe me to be, nor am I a skinflint."

"I know that," she whispered miserably, fighting down a hot wave of tears. "I'm such a spendthrift ... already spent the hundred pounds you gave me ... on *nothing*."

He leaned so close she thought he was going to grip her shoulders and shake her, but he only whispered in her ear. "And you didn't dare to confide in me? Why are you afraid of me? I should hope there's no reason to be. It distressed me to learn that you keep a secret side, as if I were an adversary. I do not like secrecy."

"What happened in the past has made it difficult for me to trust you." She swallowed a sob. "Our marriage started on a base of mistrust due to the fact that you had no desire to marry me. You did the honorable thing, but I wasn't your choice."

"We have to start building something for our marriage to stand on."

Silence stretched breathless. Allegra wondered in what sphere his thoughts were traveling. "You want us to ... to start over?"

He nodded and pulled her head down to his shoulder. "It's the only way."

"If love is not part of the marriage, we *can't* find a new start." His nearness overwhelmed her, his masculine scent, the very strength of him as he dared to touch the wound that festered under the smooth surface of their lives. She wished she could throw herself into his arms and bare her very soul.

"Yes, love is important. Trust is even more. If you can't trust me with your problems, it will be difficult to start over."

Allegra jerked away. "Don't blame me for our shortcomings, Wyndham. I did not love another when we met at the altar of St. George's."

He grew silent, and Allegra eased away from him. They traveled across Mayfair, an awkward tension hanging between them.

"You're right," he said at last, his voice hoarse with emotion. "I did love another, but now—well, I might have discovered that what I judged as love really wasn't. The values that I cherish had no place in that relationship."

She waited in silence for him to go on.

"Justine is a sparkling sun that throws bewitching rays on everyone she meets. I admit, I was dazzled. She craves a life full of excitement and variation, heady surprises, and soaring passions. To move into her realm of gaiety is inspiring, but—" He chuckled ruefully. "She inspires gentlemen to create poems to her beauty, forces one to look at the wonder of creation, coaxes one to look inside and find the ever passionate poet who lives by the smiles of goddesses and the nectar of creation."

Allegra laughed, and he slew his head around to look at her in the weak light of the lantern outside the door.

"You sounded so very melodramatic," she said.

He chuckled softly. "The hours in Justine's company *were* pure melodrama."

"And you—?"

"And I am at heart a prosaic fellow—both feet on the ground. Writing poetry at all hours was deuced taxing if you want to know the truth. I find the cares of ordinary life more rewarding than smoldering glances." He moved over to the corner where she huddled.

"In fact, I like the idea of a soft-boiled egg for breakfast, moderate starch in my collars, and the sheer pleasure of coming home to a sparkling house and cheerful servants—even if they are reformed pickpockets and circus performers." He pulled her into his arms. "Actually, I rather cherish coming home to my young wife, who shows so much talent for making everyone happy." He murmured the last words, pulling her ever closer in a heated embrace.

"I shall see that you get a draft to cover any debts, Allegra. I wish you would confide in me, if there are any problems. I don't understand why you're so reluctant to place your problems in my hands."

Seeing the Wyndham Diamonds in her mind, she stiffened and pulled away. "I have nothing to hide! There's nothing to worry your head about," she blurted out and warded off his seduction with her hands. "I don't need anything—only peace of mind."

He moved aside hesitantly. "I had hoped you would be pleased with my revelations, the truth that I don't love Justine any longer."

Allegra chewed on her bottom lip. If she let him into her heart now, confessing her own love, he would be doubly horrified if he ever discovered the truth about her underhanded dealings with Giles. He would shun her if he found out that she'd gone behind his back. "I am pleased," she said tentatively, "but you startled me with your confession. You have to give me time to consider the implications of this."

He bore an expression of outrage. "So that you'll have time to decide whether I'm worth your love or not?"

"Do not twist my words, I beg." She trembled inside and wished she could throw herself into his arms, but her problems with Giles loomed between them. There could be no secrets if their marriage was ever going to work.

"I get nothing in return for my painful revelations?" he asked incredulously.

She steeled herself. "You get a lighter heart," she whispered. "That is worth something."

He sat so very still, and she regretted her cruel words. Now was the time to confess her "sins," to reveal her lack of trust in him, and beg him to forgive her, but she could not find the courage to open her mouth.

chapter 14

They entered the Berkley Square mansion in icy silence. Francis held the door for them and gazed at Allegra as if asking what was wrong. Despite the heavy feeling in her heart, she found a small smile for him.

"How was the evening, Francis? Quiet?"

"Yes ... nobbut dead silence, melady. Knocky is off, or 'e wud 'ave sung us a song maybe."

"A useless evening, I daresay," Wyndham said coldly, and Allegra flinched at the double meaning. "Knocky takes too many liberties as it is. We don't need to hear his ditties at all hours." He slapped hat and gloves into Francis's beefy hand. "Relay a message to Dogwood for a bottle of brandy. In the library."

Allegra stared at Wyndham's angry back as he walked toward his haven at the far end of the hallway. He stopped abruptly as she dragged herself up the stairs.

"Yes, I almost forgot," he said as if to himself. "Allegra!"

She froze, turning to him in apprehension. "Yes, my lord?"

"It would be in order to wear the Wyndham Diamonds at our ball. It is the perfect occasion to show off the family

165

heirloom; in fact a Wyndham tradition for our first ball of the season. I would like to see it around your neck."

Allegra swayed as if he'd delivered a blow to her jaw. *The ball would be in a week!* Giles had a week to retrieve the necklace. *Please let him get it back in time.* To have that disastrous problem solved would be a load off her shoulders—it would clear her conscience so that she could approach Wyndham without any secrets.

"Very well. It shall be my pleasure," she said tonelessly and glanced into Wyndham's daunting eyes. He scrutinized her narrowly as if sensing her inner turmoil, then went into the library, slamming the door behind him.

If he'd asked what was wrong, she might have confessed the whole despite her promise not to denounce Giles. His eyes had not offered an invitation, however. *How shall I get through this ordeal?* Too upset to relax, she paced her bedchamber. Lucy knocked on the door and slipped into the room unobtrusively. "Do not speak, Lucy!" Allegra commanded. "I have to think."

She finally decided to write a hurried note to her brother, who'd spent the last two nights at a friend's lodgings as he was loath to face Wyndham over the breakfast table every morning.

Dearest Brother, Please wait upon me at your very earliest convenience. A matter of greatest urgency!!!! Allegra. She sanded and sealed the missive with wax, then ordered Lucy to fetch Francis.

When he entered, she said, "Take this to St. James's Street and don't leave until you have delivered it into the hands of my brother." She gave Francis the missive flanked with a hard stare. "And there's no need to tell His Lordship about this."

"Yer wish is me command, me lady. Do not fear." He bowed and took himself off.

Allegra did not sleep a wink that night, and her legs

were worn with all the nervous pacing she had done during the wee hours of the morning. Her head weighed upon her neck like a lead ball, and her eyes chafed with the gritty feeling of insomnia. She could not help but cry as she looked at her ravaged face in the mirror. Not that crying would improve her looks, she thought in a bout of savage self-loathing. Why, oh, why, had she gotten embroiled in Giles's wild schemes? The answer was simple. She couldn't stand by and watch the moneylenders ruin her brother's life.

She scooped up the kitten from the bed and cradled his soft body in her arms. His friendly purr failed to cheer her this morning, and she set him down on his favorite spot— her pillows.

Giles arrived shortly after breakfast. Allegra held her finger to her lips and pointed toward the library door. She hadn't seen or heard Wyndham this morning, but she suspected he was nursing his wounded pride among his books. She beckoned her brother upstairs and pulled him into her private boudoir.

After closing the door, she whispered, "Thank heavens you came, Giles."

Her brother fingered his neckcloth nervously. "Why are you all in a lather, sis? Has Wyndham gotten wind of our scheme?"

Allegra sighed and strode across the room. She gripped a needlepoint pillow from a chair and pressed it against her middle to soothe the achy tension inside. "No, not yet, but he will if you don't retrieve the diamonds, posthaste. Giles, you *must* save me!"

"What is amiss?" Giles started pacing, too, and as they met at the center of the floor, Allegra said,

"Wyndham wants me to wear the diamonds to our ball. Don't you see, there are only a few days left." Allegra shook her brother's arm. "Do you have the funds to buy back the necklace?"

Giles brightened. "You're in luck, I do. I won a large sum yesterday, but I planned to use it to further my fortune at the card tables."

Allegra moaned. "That is a bacon-brained idea if I ever heard one! How can you even think of risking a repeat of your great loss and staking my very *future*? I am quite out of patience with you." She glared at him, pleased to see his discomfort. "I expect you to return here tonight, necklace in hand. Or I will never speak to you again."

"Point taken, sis. You don't have to glower at me like that. I am mayhap a trifle overly optimistic in my gambling, but I know when the wind is in my favor. I could double my winnings."

"Be that as it may, but I demand your cooperation in this, or I will take the whole to Wyndham and let him deal with you."

Giles recoiled visibly. "No need for that, surely. Wyndham can be deuced formidable, and I wouldn't want to be found lacking."

Allegra viewed the bags of dissipation under her brother's eyes and felt as if she were the older, more experienced sibling. So much had changed in the past months, and the weight of her new responsibilities burdened her shoulders.

"If I were you, Giles, I would return to Oxford and study hard to get through the exams successfully. You have the opportunity to educate yourself, but you idle away your nights drinking and gambling. I would dearly like to know how you managed to slink away from your studies—what kind of arrangement you set up, what lies you told. Pinkney might already be in possession of a letter that expels you from university."

Giles paled and shoved his hands through his hair. "No

need to fly into a pet over it. Well ... I was planning to return just as soon as I'd retrieved the necklace."

"That is tonight. I suggest that you book a seat on the next stagecoach north," Allegra went on inexorably. "I am not going to help you out of another scrape."

"Greek and Latin," he muttered scathingly. "Only the old codgers take interest in such drivel, and I ain't old yet." He flung himself out of the room after the merest farewell.

Allegra had a premonition of disaster, but she prayed that her senses played her wrong. Too nervous to settle down, she spent the day flitting about the house making sure the servants were preparing for the ball. There was silver to polish, tablecloths to launder, and crystal chandeliers to clean.

As evening arrived, she thought she would shatter with brittle tension. If someone spoke too harshly or too loudly, she would surely break apart like a windowpane hit by a stone.

Wyndham put in a brief appearance at the midday meal, then betook himself out of the house. He didn't speak with Allegra, only favored her with slightest of nods in greeting. *Beast!* she longed to call him, but there was no telling what he would call her in return. Better let him soothe his pride in silence. Besides, she cherished the small reprieve as she could not keep up the pretense that all was fine. She'd rather not lie to her husband, however much she resented his ill-mannered brooding.

At about seven her nerves had been strung on a rack and tightened until she could do nothing more useful than hover by the windows and stare out at the empty street.

Dull clouds had gathered across the sky, a light drizzle rapidly increasing to a steady rainfall. Silver streaks meandered down the glass panes, distorting her view of the square. Finally a hack stopped by the door. A gentleman emerged and rushed up the steps to bang on the door.

Allegra ran to the hallway. Xerxes, wearing his newly acquired haughty expression, probably inspired by Dogwood, let in her soggy brother. He handed his hat and gloves to the footman, and brushed rain from the shoulders. "A perishing night, sis." He was wearing a hideous pink waistcoat of brocaded satin and a moss-green double-breasted coat. The colors gave Allegra a headache.

"I thought you would never come!" she admonished.

Giles looked hopefully toward the dining room. "Is dinner ready? I'm sharp set."

"I did not invite you for dinner, Giles," she said, but relented as she noticed his hungry expression. "Oh, very well, I asked for a cold collation brought to the breakfast parlor. Wyndham is dining out."

She glanced at his coat for any telltale bulges of the hidden necklace but found none. Worry intensified inside her, and she urged her brother into the nearest salon.

"Where is it?" she whispered.

Giles closed the door softly to prevent any lurking servants from overhearing their conversation. "I ain't got it, sis."

Allegra gasped and stared at him in horror. "You don't have it with you? Why? Did you forget it at your friend's lodgings?"

He flung out his arms, an expression of deep chagrin spreading on his face. "I didn't forget it, sis! There's nothing wrong with my memory."

With clammy hands, Allegra gripped the back of a chair and waited for him to go on. She visualized deep trouble ahead.

"Sally Spinks, that double-faced witch, she wouldn't let me have the dashed necklace," he blurted out, his voice laced with disgust. "She's developed greedy fingers since she started that school of Venus. Didn't used to be such a harridan, y'know."

"School of Venus?" Puzzled, Allegra stared at him. "What is this woman's profession? I thought she was a friend of yours."

Giles shuffled his feet uneasily. "Well ... yes, sort of." He cleared his throat noisily. "She fences stolen items and also lends money to valued customers. Don't charge much interest, but she's demanding another five hundred pounds to relinquish the necklace. Seems she knows it's very valuable."

"My God!" Allegra groaned and sank down on the chair. "Whatever shall we do?"

"I don't have a penny to my name, sis. Gave her the two thousand and asked for the necklace when she came the ugly with me." Giles slumped into a chair and propped his elbows on his knees. He lowered his head into his hands and moaned. "By thunder I should not have given her the four monkeys before I had the necklace safely in my hand."

Allegra stared at her brother in surprise. "What are you talking about? Monkeys?"

"A monkey is five-hundred pounds, sis. Oh, it's a damned nuisance! I'm ruined. If I'd held back some blunt, I would have had enough to make another try at the tables."

"If you go back with another five hundred, she'll probably ask for more. Oh, Giles, we *must* retrieve the necklace." Allegra struggled against the tears pooling into her eyes. Gloomy silence fell in the room, the only sound the patter of rain on window glass.

She started with fear as someone suddenly sneezed in the shadows by the terrace door. The movement had come from a large armchair. *Wyndham?* Please God, don't let it be Wyndham, she prayed frantically, staring mesmerized at the chair.

" 'Tis only me, melady," came Knocky's cheerful voice.

"What in the world! Are you spying on us, Knocky?"

"No ... melady, but I wus uneasy 'bout revealin' meself, thinkin' as I've been sleepin' in Yer Ladyship's chair. I 'ad no mind for a tongue-lashin'."

"Oh, how could you! His Lordship will whip you when he returns," Allegra said and glared at her brother, who was chuckling.

"Naw, 'e don't use whips. Does not need to. 'Is tongue is much sharper, and a whuppin' wi' that is worse than th' cat o' nines." Knocky didn't sound overly concerned, and Allegra longed to take the whip to him right then and there. Her patience sorely tried all day, she lashed out. "You're not to have any days off for the next two months, Knocky. Dogwood shall work you to the bone."

" 'E stays away from me whenever 'e can. I suppose I smell bad or sumthin'."

" 'Tis your uncouth tongue that provokes Dogwood's nerves, I'll wager, and your unbridled singing at all hours. Come here," Allegra ordered.

Knocky stood before his mistress, livery wrinkled and hair hanging lank and unbrushed around his face.

"You look a disgrace, Knocky. You ought to have a bath, and I shall send for Xerxes—"

"Wait, sis! I've got an idea." Laughing, Giles stood and kicked up his heels. "We shall *steal* the necklace from Sally Spinks. After all, I repaid the loan, so she owes me."

"Are we to break into her house and take it?" Allegra gaped in surprise.

"Yes!" Giles stared benevolently at Knocky. "And Knocky shall help us. That'll be his punishment for sleeping during work hours." He shook the boy's shoulder. "After all, he's up to every rig in the business of stealing, ain't you, Knocky."

"Stealin'?" Knocky asked wide-eyed. "I've never nimmed as much as a silk 'andkerchief."

"This will be the first time, then," Giles said with a wink. "Small of body that you are, you'll be the one to whisk into Sally's lair and grab the diamonds."

Knocky looked at Allegra with misgiving. "Do I 'avta do what the spark says? Go into the moll's 'ouse and ransack her valuables?"

"No, not exactly," Giles said with great patience.

Allegra stood, wanting to wash her hands of the whole business. "If you can help my brother, then you shall, Knocky. There's no other solution."

The boy whined. "Ow, but stealin' is a 'angin' matter. I don't need me neck stretched."

"We shan't get caught, you clodhopper."

Knocky gave Giles a surly glance. " 'Tis you who is touched in yer upper works, Mister Temple."

Giles rubbed his hands in glee, not at all disturbed by the slur upon his character. "We must sit down and plan the whole."

chapter 15

"*I* can't do that!" Allegra exclaimed, aghast at the suggestion that she stand watch for the lawbreakers.

"It ain't dangerous. All you have to do—in the protection of your carriage—is make sure no one is going into the house as we break in."

Allegra shivered with unease and glowered at her brother. "It's unthinkable. In fact, you put us in this situation, Giles, and you shall find a way to retrieve the necklace without my help."

He continued as if not listening. "When Sally leaves the house next, that'll be the time we strike."

Knocky scratched his head in thought. "What 'bout th' other bits of muslin? They live at the Spinks woman's house. There day an' night."

Giles laughed as if enjoying his plan hugely. "You're right! I knew you would be familiar with the problems facing our larcenous mission, Knocky."

Knocky pursed his lips in thought and shifted his feet. "I don't know. There's Sally's door in bold view. I ain't no rum dubber."

"You don't need to pick the lock. I'll hoist you in through the window."

Allegra fought a bout of faintness as she listened to

these wild plans. Giles talked about breaking in as if were a walk in the park. She pressed her handkerchief to her temples as if to steady herself. As the parlor door opened softly, she jumped with guilt. She froze as she spied her husband in the doorway.

"Wyndham! You decided to come home for dinner, after all," she said, her mouth full of false cheerfulness.

"Good evening," her husband said and leaned against the doorframe. His gaze slid from person to person, lingering on Knocky. Allegra blushed and averted her eyes. "What a dashing gathering. Am I invited?"

Evidently his ill humor had disappeared, and Allegra wished she could rush into his arms and beg his forgiveness for her callous behavior in the coach. "Of course. I shall ask Dogwood to arrange for dinner in half an hour."

He strolled inside, and Knocky slid out from the room without so much as a sound. "You seem as thick as thieves," the earl drawled and scrutinized Giles's heated face.

"I should hope not," Allegra snapped, trying to hide her guilt with a display of arrogance. "Giles is merely paying me a brotherly visit before going back to Oxford."

"I have noticed your frequent visits to Brook's, Giles. I understand that the tables hold great interest, but I must say, however, that I'm surprised you've chosen such deep play as transpires at the club. I surmise you have deep pockets, or dashed good luck."

Giles threw a hasty glance at Allegra. "My sister is not the only Temple who is lucky. Some of the magic has rubbed off on me."

Wyndham glanced from one to the other suspiciously. He sat down, swinging one leg over the other. Wearing light gray pantaloons and a coat of blue superfine, he was the picture of a sophisticated member of the *haut ton*.

Allegra's heart ached as she thought about the barrier she'd erected between them.

"Are you implying that you, like Allegra, found a four-leaf clover on Temple land?" Wyndham's lips quirked upward, as he continued. "Mayhap Sir Edwin cultivated them. You might show me the spot someday so that I can find the luck—and have my most urgent wish fulfilled." He gave Allegra a pointed glance, and she knew he was referring to their argument in the coach after the Duchess of Newberry's ball. She cringed under the burden of guilt.

Wyndham got up suddenly and sauntered to the sofa where she was sitting. He leaned over her, and she ducked her head, staring at her lap as the tension built between them.

"I would dearly like to look at that four-leaf clover, if you don't mind," he drawled in her ear.

His presence demanded that she look up into his silver-blue eyes where a haunted quality darkened the irises to a deep charcoal. She sensed his longing for her and was humbled by the realization that she had the power to touch his heart. If only Giles hadn't embroiled himself with some unsavory character who even now might be in the process of selling the Wyndham Diamonds! Wyndham would be excessively angry if he discovered the truth.

He touched the locket pinned right above her left breast. "May I?"

The heat of his fingers penetrated the thin cambric of her gown, and she flinched away. Steeling herself against the onslaught of emotions, she pinched the spring that opened the lid of her locket. "There. See for yourself—Ian."

Under glass, a four-leaf clover was pinned to a white velvet background, all leaves attached to the stem. "It is not a regular clover with an extra leaf," she said with some asperity.

"I can see that," Wyndham said. He leaned closer to get a better look. His breath fanned her cheek, and she had a feeling he could look straight into her rotten—racing—heart.

Her lips stiff with tension, she said, "The four leaves stand for different things: one for fame, another for wealth, one for good health . . . and—"

"The last one?" he queried, as if already knowing the answer.

"One for a faithful—lover," she said with a gulp and looked away.

"Ah! I daresay you have them all, especially—fame, after the musicale evening."

"And she lives in clover," Giles added readily.

Allegra wished she sat close enough to kick his shin.

Wyndham whispered into her ear. "The lover issue is as yet unsettled, but I expect the fourth prophecy shall be taken care of in time."

Allegra forced a smile to her lips. "Only time will tell." She thought he would kiss her right then and there, but he wouldn't act so gauche as to display emotions outside the boudoir. He didn't. He straightened slowly and snapped the lid closed. She jumped as if slapped.

"As long as time is not eternity," he murmured and went back to his chair.

Giles sprang to his feet and fiddled nervously with his shirt cuffs. "I suppose 'tis *time* for me to leave you two lovebirds alone."

"I have a distinct feeling you're trying to avoid me, Temple. I would like some gesture that you don't find my presence distasteful. May I offer you a glass of port, perhaps?"

Allegra sensed the vise tightening around the situation. Evidently her husband could tell that Giles had visited with no intention of paying respects to his brother-in-law.

In fact, it looked as if he'd chosen a time to visit when Wyndham was out. Did Wyndham sniff their underhanded secret in the air?

Guilt blanketed Giles face and a flush suffused his face with red. "Most obliged to you, Wyndham, but I have a prior engagement." He bowed and turned toward Allegra. She feared he would make some frantic sign, but he said or did nothing, only bussed her cheek and hurried out the door.

"He left as if fire lapped at his heels," Wyndham said dryly.

Allegra tried to lighten the mood. "I believe he finds our situation rather boring. No gambling, no carousing, no lounging in Bond Street. If anything, Giles is a man about town—or likes to think he is."

"Like all greenheads, a man of more hair than wit." Wyndham hauled out his snuffbox and glanced at her speculatively. She noticed that he was using the one she'd given him.

"You are very young, Allegra. I daresay you would like a more spirited environment than being ensconced in this *boring* situation," he said.

"Have you heard me complain?" Allegra replied with a genuine smile. "I thoroughly enjoy my domestic responsibilities, and I am looking forward to traveling to High Wyndham once the season is over."

The tension left his face, and a smile took its place. With the change, Allegra could draw a deep sigh of relief. "It will be a pleasure to breathe country air again." He rose. "Come, let's go and see if dinner is served." He held out his arm to her, and as she hooked his elbow, he patted her hand reassuringly.

"I think you not afraid of me any longer, wife."

Allegra blushed and lowered her gaze. "Mayhap not as much. There's no reason to be."

"I would so very much like to consummate our marriage," he whispered as they reached the door.

Allegra noted his hopeful expression, and she curbed her feeling of panic. Giving him a wobbly smile, she said, "You flatter me, my lord—Ian. Maybe it is time. Soon."

Allegra waited nervously with Knocky at the entrance of the Wyndham mansion. "Do you think he'll come?" she asked for the tenth time. She glanced at the clock in the corner, noting the minutes pass at a snail's pace.

" 'E'll be 'ere. Tonight is our only chance to git that damned necklace outta that school of Venus in Russell Street. Sally and 'er gels are at Bagnigge Wells offerin' their wares to the dandy prats, I'll lay."

Allegra had deduced that the "school" was no better than a house of ill repute. She recoiled at the thought of her husband's gift in the hands of a Fallen Woman. Wyndham would be furious if he found out, and find out he would if Giles didn't appear soon. Only two hours remained until their guests started to arrive for the ball. She could think of nothing else.

Unseeing, Allegra viewed the high ceiling and the garlands of flowers with which she'd decorated the doors to the ballroom upstairs. Candles blazed, and every surface had been washed and polished, including the picture frames. Her home glittered and buzzed in the expectation of guests.

Two hours. After that it would be too late. She was wearing an ice-blue, empire-style silk gown with a row of flounces, bodice tucks, and a daring neckline, to set off the Wyndham Diamonds. Her new slippers pinched her toes, and her hands perspired in the confines of fine elbow-length silk gloves. Shivering with worry, she touched her bare neck, noticing that a curl had come loose from the hair arrangement adorned with diamond aigrettes.

"Have you seen His Lordship this evening, Knocky?"

"No, melady. I believe 'e's upstairs dressin'. That namby-pamby, Oglesby, 'ot-footed upstairs with a stack o' clean neckcloths, not an 'our past."

Finally the sounds of wheels and trotting horses reached her ears. "That must be Giles. Go see, Knocky."

"Drivin' at neck-or-nothin', no doubt." The page obeyed, stepping out onto the front steps. He nodded, waved at her, and ran down to the waiting coach. Allegra touched her locket and prayed that all would go well.

Giles Temple was not one to avoid larks of any kind, but this latest escapade smacked of real danger. He might hang for breaking into a house. But it was too late now to contemplate any other venues to restoring the blasted necklace.

"Guv, if ye don't mind me sayin' so, I don't expecially care for this outin'. I've been 'appy as a grig wi' 'Er Ladyship, an' I don't much like th' thought o' losin' me 'igh place in the world. I don't fancy findin' meself at Newman's 'Otel, either, if ye see what I means."

Giles snorted. "You ain't going to end up in Newgate, Knocky. We'll dash in, find the gems, and get out. No one the wiser." Despite his cheerful optimism, Giles inserted his finger under the too tight collar and tried to ease the pressure. "We'll do this as planned. You on my shoulders, and in through the window. I went to see Sally yesterday and managed to open a window latch on my way out. If she didn't notice, we should get in easily."

"Unless some'un made it there first. There are gangs wot mill the kens in ten minutes and take off wi' all th' silver. Wot with an open winder, well—" Knocky heaved his shoulders in a speaking shrug.

"Don't be so glum," Giles barked with more strength

than he felt inside. He gulped down a surge of fear. "We'll be back in no time at all."

Russell Street on the east side of Covent Garden echoed with rowdy altercations and high-pitched laughter as the evening activities came into full swing. Gambling hells and popular coffee houses drew customers from all walks of life. Carriages and hackney cabs trundled along the cobbled street, gas lamps attached to the vehicles illuminating the faces of pleasure-seeking young blades clinging to women of dubious character. Theatergoers mingled with flower sellers, and raucous voices rose toward the overcast sky. Sally Spinks's house brooded at the far end, in the corner. It was a tall parsimonious house with a brick wall encasing a small garden plot at the back.

Giles paid the jarvey and pushed Knocky toward the wall without ado.

"Aaoo, guv, yer pinchin' me arm," the boy whined. His gaze darted around the area knowingly. "I 'ope ye know what yer doin, Mr. Temple."

"Be quiet, Knocky." Giles pulled the small page with him into the shadows. "I'm going to lift you up onto the wall. The unlatched window is the one at the end. You should be able to get in easily."

Knocky swore under his breath as Giles hoisted the boy onto his shoulders. The page scrambled onto the wall, and walked quickly along the bricks to the window in question. A watchman carrying lantern and staff came into view, and Giles pressed himself against the wall so as not to be seen. In the blink of an eye, Knocky crouched, making himself melt with the shadows. Giles drew a sigh of relief at Knocky's deft act.

The boy got up and tried the window as soon as the charlie had passed. Giles peered anxiously around as he heard the window creak loudly. There was no one loitering nearby. He took a step back, just in time to see Knocky's legs wiggling through the narrow opening. So far, so good! If only they could find the necklace. They would, as long as it had not been removed from the premises. . . . Giles swallowed hard at that thought. What if Sally had already sold the necklace for a small fortune? He'd been a fool to trust her! But she had acted as his friend who was willing to help him in a pinch. That was before she showed her true colors. *I was daft to believe her sugary promises,* Giles thought, remembering (not without longing) her pouting red lips, soft bosom, and plump inviting limbs.

A silver-tongued witch, no more, no less. He waited anxiously for Knocky to come downstairs and unlock the back door. He did, five minutes later, and let Giles in through the rough gate in the wall.

"You took your time," Giles hissed.

"Can't see nubbut in the dark. No one at 'ome 'xept the cat. A scratchin' and bitin' little divil." Knocky sucked on his hand and led the way into the house. They didn't waste time finding Sally's boudoir cum office on the second floor.

"I'll look in the desk. You can start searching for the strongbox," Giles said, pulling out drawers. He found nothing but broken quills, yellowed paper, and gobs of red wax. A pair of black net gloves resided among the debris. Nothing of value here, he thought.

"Found th' box, guv," Knocky said excitedly from under the bed. "As 'eavy as Sally's arse," he elucidated.

Giles chuckled and helped Knocky lift the chest onto the desk. With eager hands, he jangled the spring lock, but it did not budge.

"We could take the whole thing," Knocky said in a hopeful voice.

"A pea-brained idea. Have you forgotten that you're now treading the narrow path of an honest man?"

"No ... guv." Knocky licked his lips and started attacking the lock with a letter opener. It wouldn't open.

As steps echoed along the street outside, Giles looked frantically for a tool to apply. He couldn't find anything sturdy enough. "Blast and damn!"

They spent twenty nerve-racking minutes on the lock, which had been made by a master blacksmith no doubt. Giles's nerves had frayed to tatters.

"I'm going downstairs to look for a mallet or something equally heavy. No use to dawdle here. Someone might hear us," Giles said and sprinted down the stairs. He feared the ladies of easy virtue would come through the front door at any minute now.

He found nothing in the kitchen. Entering the scullery through a narrow foul-smelling corridor, he came upon an ax that evidently was used for cutting splinters for kindling. He hefted it and retraced his steps.

He thought he heard running footsteps outside. The sound urged him to greater speed. "Here, let's try this," he shouted in a whisper as he entered the boudoir. Confused, he looked around the empty room.

"Dang it all, where are you hiding, Knocky? No time for games." He walked across the floor scanning every corner for the playful page. No sign of the jester.

His gaze fell on the open strongbox. *Open!* By Gad, they hadn't managed to break the lock, so what—? In the faint light coming from the street, he looked at the contents strewn over the table, Cheap necklaces, bracelets, coins, earrings, some more valuable than others. Among the welter of gems, he could not find the Wyndham Diamonds. He slammed down the ax onto the desk and swore a long harangue. "Damn that flea-ridden pickpocket! I'll see his neck strung up in the gallows for this."

To cover his tracks, he shoved the jewelry back into the strongbox and pushed it under the bed. After returning the ax to the scullery, he sneaked out the kitchen door—just like that good-for-nothing page must have done only moments ago. He glanced in both directions of the street in hope of seeing the fleeing boy. Nothing. Not a soul anywhere close by. "Damn it all to hell!"

After reaching the street, he ought to feel weak with relief, but worry was nibbling ever faster at his composure. What in the world was he to tell Allegra? She would be livid. Who could blame her?

He hastened along the street, not noticing the crowds outside the gin shops, or the beggars that cried out in plaintive voices. All he could think of was the ordeal of meeting his sister with the terrible news.

Maybe he should leave, fading out of London like a thief. He curbed the thought to buy a ticket on the first stagecoach leaving from the White Stag. He couldn't very well leave Allegra to face her intimidating husband alone.

Allegra waited, and waited. Time had never moved more slowly. Her brother was bound to arrive any minute with the necklace in his pocket. Why was it that she doubted him, doubted his ability to handle this difficult dilemma?

She stood by the window in the blue salon, and when she saw Giles half running up the street, she dropped the blue velvet drapes in place and sat down by the fireplace, staring into the empty grate.

No more had he knocked on the door before he flung himself inside the room under Dogwood's startled stare. He looked disheveled, his hair mussed, and his hands dirty as if he'd worked all evening. Which he probably had.

He slammed the door in Dogwood's face.

"You arrived in time, thank God. I have been so nervous," Allegra said with a laugh of relief and went eagerly toward him, her hands outstretched. "Where is it? I take it you succeeded?"

"That blasted hedge-bird of a page! I could tie him behind a mad horse. That should teach him to show some respect!"

Allegra gasped, stilling her movements. Her heart sank as she realized that the mission had been a failure. "What about Knocky? What has he done?"

"He ran away with the dratted necklace, that's what he did! I swear I'll string him up by his thumbs and whip some sense into him. That is if I ever clap eyes on him again."

"Ohhh, this is the worst bumblebroth— My God, whatever shall we do? The guests will arrive shortly, and I promised—"

He collapsed into a chair. "Why, Wyndham might have forgotten his request, sis."

She shook her head. "No, he'll stress that it is tradition to wear the diamonds at the Wyndham House ball." She wrung her hands. "I tremble in my slippers at the thought of confessing the whole to him. He will be so very angry. He will loathe me."

"There is nothing for it, sis, but to take the bull by the horns. You'll have to own up." He hung his head and grimaced. Appearing much younger than his nineteen years, he added, "I'll lend you my support, and mayhap he won't blame you for the disaster. The blame lies wholly with me."

"I know, but I agreed to help you. We should have gone to Wyndham in the first—"

The door opened slowly and the earl stood on the threshold, his eyebrows raised in question. "I thought I heard your voices in here, and noted a decidedly worried tone. Is there a problem?" Wyndham stepped inside, handsome in a dark green coat with gold buttons, a waistcoat of gold brocade, knee breeches, and evening shoes.

Allegra exchanged a worried look with Giles. Her brother wore an expression of despair, as if he was about to step up to the gallows, the next ruffian to hang. In comparison with her sophisticated, and always in control, husband, Giles looked like a callow schoolboy.

Wyndham stopped in front of Giles and stared down at him. "What have you done, Temple? I dare swear you're behind the agitated whispering."

Giles straightened his slumped shoulders. "You're correct, Wyndham. I have been foolish to enmesh Allegra in one of my nefarious schemes."

Wyndham gave Allegra a penetrating glance, and she wished the floor would open up and she would fall into oblivion. "Well?"

"Ahem!" Giles cleared his throat noisily and darted a worried glance at Allegra. She could only nod to urge him into the tale, even if it would paint her both ungrateful, deceitful, and mistrustful.

"I . . . well, you see, I entered a game of cards in Oxford and lost some funds." He took a deep breath. "In fact, my entire allowance for the year, and . . . a lot more, earlier gambling wins." Giles had paled and drops of perspiration had gathered on his brow. "More like two thousand pounds."

An incredulous silence fell, then slowly grew heavier as Wyndham's anger started to rise in his face. His jaw tightened, and his lips thinned to a stern line. "I take it you couldn't pay off your debt," he said in a flat voice.

Giles nodded miserably. "I didn't know what to do, so I borrowed from the cents-per-cent, and you know how inflated their interest becomes. I had to pay the first installment a week after the game, but my pockets were bare. I lost my luck at the tables. The only solution I could think of was traveling to London—"

"—and crying for help at your sister's door?" Wyndham filled in, his voice deadly.

"Yes ... well, I thought she would have some funds, her allowance, y'know, but—" Giles stopped abruptly and turned a guilty eye on Allegra.

She sighed, fearing to look into Wyndham's eyes, as she spoke. "I'd spent every penny, but we decided to borrow money against the diamond necklace and pay off the usurers."

Wyndham's eyes darkened with fury. "So you thought so little of me that you couldn't come to me with the problem?" he asked in that icy soft voice.

"We ... I didn't want to worry you," Allegra said. "You would have been very angry with me for squandering my money so quickly. And understandably so."

"I am a stern disciplinarian and a clutch-fist, is that it?" Wyndham asked scathingly. "I would think you had better sense than to listen to your brother and his woes." He turned to Giles. "And you, sirrah, should have approached me instead of dragging your sister through this scurrilous ordeal."

"Yes, sir, I understand," Giles muttered. "But this isn't the whole of it." He launched into the story of Sally Spinks, the two thousand pounds he paid her, and his consequent evening visit to Sally's empty house. As an afterthought he mentioned Knocky's deceit and final desertion.

Allegra saw that Wyndham was struggling hard to keep his fury under control. He flexed his hands as if longing to clasp his strong fingers around someone's neck and squeeze. He marched around the perimeter of the room, and Allegra waited anxiously for the storm that was bound to erupt.

He finally stopped in front of Giles. His words came out like whip lashes. "I hope this has taught you a lesson, Temple. Don't play any deeper than you can afford, and don't visit the moneylenders again. Next time you are in a scrape, come to see me. *Do not* lay the burden on your sister! Very ungentlemanly thing to do." He thought for a moment. "I expect to hear that you're back in Oxford by tomorrow night, or I shall be obliged to inform Pinkney of your appalling adventures. And I don't want to hear rumors that you're exchanging your studies for gambling. If I do, I shall make life very difficult for you." He gripped Giles shoulder and shook it. "It's time to grow up, Temple, and shoulder your responsibilities as a man."

Giles flinched at every rule laid down and bobbed his head nervously. He fingered his neckcloth and touched his fiery red cheeks as the earl let go. "Yes, my lord."

Allegra wanted to plead with her husband, but Wyndham turned his back and marched out of the room without as much as a glance at her.

"Whew! I was reduced to shortcoats, sis. Flayed me as hard as Father's rakedowns used to."

"You needed one! I daresay you wouldn't act like a rakehell if Father were still alive."

"I suppose not," Giles said, shoulders slumping.

"You can't trifle with Wyndham. You'd better obey him, or he'll never trust you again," Allegra said, feeling miserable. "He won't ever trust *me* after this. I didn't trust him enough to lay my problems before him."

Giles straightened his back and heaved a deep sigh. "Nonsense! I'm glad this ordeal is over at last. My conscience feels lighter by far." A new determination set his jaw. "Wyndham is right. I'll have to take full responsibility for this. I shall take myself off to search for that scoundrel, Knocky, and when I find him, I shall drag him here by his ear." Giles kissed Allegra's cheek, and she didn't have the strength to argue further. The evening that had barely started was already a disaster.

Wearing the sapphires Wyndham had given her, she greeted the guests, her husband icily silent beside her.

chapter 16

Allegra didn't know how she got through the evening, smiling and chatting as if nothing was amiss. Wyndham treated her as if she didn't exist, but played the perfect host to the guests that had come to dance and eat lobster patties, salmon in aspic, tarts, creams, and jellies, and washing it all down with the finest champagne.

By the small hours her head pounded with a vicious headache, and her cheeks ached from all the forced smiles. If only she could bare her heart to Wyndham, make him see that she'd been too afraid to approach him with her problems. He had always intimidated her, but she had come to understand the man, a kind and humorous and rather lonely fellow behind the sophisticated facade. Lately, they had shared and reached out, tentatively touching each other's hearts, treading a path as fragile as eggshells.

She had crushed everything with her mistrust.

Allegra waved to the last guests leaving the mansion. If she didn't soon reach her chamber, she feared she would collapse with the strain of keeping up a cheerful mien. She drew a sigh of relief as she dashed upstairs to seek the haven of her bedchamber.

With longing, and dark pain flowing in his heart, Wyndham watched her slender back as she ran for shelter. A small defenseless rabbit, but harboring the wily mind of a fox. Why had she not divulged her problems to him?

Why? The question burned in his mind until he thought he was going to smash something, an old Oriental vase, perhaps, or the priceless china. It would feel damned good to slam his fist into something and see it break.

Had she so little trust in him that she couldn't confide her monetary problems? Money meant so little when there were deeper emotional questions unanswered. He didn't give a damn if she squandered half of his fortune on fripperies! Incomprehensible, he thought and demanded his hat and gloves from Francis, who was waiting by the door and following him with worried eyes.

"Right away, guv. Lor'ship, I means." He returned posthaste. "Goin' out at this time o' night, me lord?"

"Yes, nothing for you to worry about, Francis."

"I wouldn't mind accompanying ye fer a walk, me lord. I'll keep well behind if ye want."

Wyndham scrutinized the substantial man for a moment. "Very well. Come along. We're going into the warrens of St. Giles."

Francis's eyes widened. "Cor, me lord!" He ripped off his powdered wig and placed it on the floor, then started unbuttoning the livery.

Wyndham watched the servant with amusement. "What are you doing, Francis?"

"Can't very well go into the rookeries dressed as a popinjay. The roughs'll 'ave me stripped in no time, and rolled in tar."

"That's right. Better dress in your regular clothes. I'll wait here." He pointed at the wig. "Better take that with you, or that rascally cat might think it's an intruder of the feline kind."

Francis's face broke open in a grin. "Yer right, guv. Be back in a trice."

The air of the rookeries north of the City hung foul with the odors of refuse, stale food and beer, and urine. Wyndham wrinkled his fastidious nose. Strange that he as a young buck about town—not that many years ago really—had found such amusement in low taverns and disreputable gaming hells. Like Giles now. Any dangerous lark, the more dangerous the better, sparked among his friends, had sent them out carousing through dark alleyways and courtyards where footpads and murderers lurked.

He visited a tavern on Long Lane owned by Big Charlie, a former pugilist who had looked too deeply into the bottle too long. He knew, however, all the gossip of the underworld. Big Charlie was a fence, and he'd bought two rings from Wyndham once when the earl had been in the same predicament as Giles. Wyndham shook his head with disgust as the remembered the follies of his first year in town. Like Giles, he hadn't dared to ask his father for a loan. Wyndham hoped Giles had learned something from this latest scrape and would curb some of his wilder activities.

Wyndham gave a grim smile and stepped into the gin-soaked air of the tavern. The low ceiling sagged in the middle, giving the impression it was ready to cave in. Rowdies wrangled and drank from their tankards, and Wyndham had to step over sprawling legs of customers who were well over the oar.

Wyndham spotted Big Charlie behind the bar, leaning his elbows on the greasy counter beside a fat ale barrel. Wishing he could hold his breath against the fetid aromas, Wyndham marched up to the proprietor. If anyone, Big Charlie would know if the diamonds had been sold in the last few hours.

Big Charlie glared at him with rheumy eyes. His fleshy face had a pasty tinge, and the bulbous nose a decidedly purple cast. He slapped a meaty fist on the counter as he recognized Wyndham. "Ain't bin 'round 'ere in a long time, guv. Don't like the company?" He laughed, showing a row of rotten teeth.

A drunkard gripped Wyndham's arm to haul himself upright, but Francis chopped downward at the grimy fist. "Keep yer fives ter yerself," he growled.

"I'm a married man now, Charlie. Can't jaunt about town at night." He fished a guinea from the deep pocket of his greatcoat and shoved it across the counter. "Here, give me a glass of blue ruin. I hope you no longer serve the rotgut you used to."

Big Charlie scooped up the coin and studied it thoughtfully. "I serve only th' best, guv, but it ain't worth a goldfinch." He drew his heavy eyebrows together and glowered at Wyndham. "Wot do ye want?" While waiting for an answer, he filled a glass and pushed it across the counter. A tallow candle flickered in the wake of his movement, casting devilish shadows on the craggy face.

"My wife's page took off with the family jewels, Charlie. Have you heard anything about a fine diamond necklace gone astray lately?" Wyndham swept up the glass and downed the contents, the fiery liquid forcing him to gasp for breath.

Big Charlie shook his head and leaned nonchalantly on the bar. "Ain't 'eard nuthin'. Ain't likely the diamonds will remain a collar, nohow."

Hot wrath spread through Wyndham. He slowly leaned over the counter and gripped the front of Big Charlie's grimy shirt. Twisting it, he pulled the large man toward him. The din in the room slowly stilled to awed silence. "How much do you want, Charlie? I need the information."

Charlie's meaty fist clenched and unclenched, and the crowd seemed to expect him to plant a facer to the nob's face. Francis moved in closer, but not too close.

Wyndham and Charlie stood locked in a battle of wills, and finally Charlie averted his gaze and slowly pried the earl's hand from his shirt. "Five goldfinches and we'll try again," he muttered.

As the earl loosened his grip, the crowd returned to their erstwhile conversations. Wyndham brought up a leather purse and tossed it in front of Big Charlie. The pugilist buried it in his fist. "Last I 'ear, Mrs. Spinks's 'ouse wus looted. Lost a string of diamonds. Not likely 'er can afford sparklers like that, I says to meself. But she raised the divil's own row. Sum'one saw bloomin' Knocky Martin sneak outta 'er 'ouse. Says 'e's back on th' streets, and Mrs. Spinks 'as sent 'er boys arter 'im. Knocky ain't long for this world, I reckon."

Wyndham narrowed his eyes. "Are you saying Knocky hasn't been caught, and that no one has bought diamonds this evening?"

"Tha's God's truth."

Wyndham slapped his hand down hard on the pitted wood. "You send word when you know what's happened. I want those diamonds, and I'm willing to pay well. You'll get five percent of the deal."

"Ten, guv, an' you 'ave a deal."

The earl shrugged. "Very well. But listen here, the moment you hear anything, let me know."

Wyndham's gaze swept the drinkers in the gloomy room, as if expecting to see Knocky's leering face, but Knocky would be too clever to linger where he could be seen.

If I get to him before the Spinks woman does, he will get a hiding the like he has never seen, the earl thought and marched out the door.

He visited two other similar taverns, but the news was always the same. Knocky Martin had disappeared, and so had the Wyndham Diamonds.

As dawn neared, the earl stepped into a hackney and ordered the driver to take him to Russell Street. Francis jumped up at the back, and the hack lurched forward.

Wyndham pondered the mystery of Knocky's disappearance, and a dark anger settled over him. Had he been too indulging to allow such a jailbird as Knocky Martin to make his home at Berkley Square? He had not seen any harm in it except for the outrage shown by his starchier servants. However, according to Mrs. Buxton, the boy had made friends with most of the staff and had brought an air of cheerfulness to the nether regions of his house. Even Dogwood was coming around. However, would a thief change his ways? Hardly likely.

The hack stopped in front of Mrs. Spinks's house, and Wyndham jumped down, closely followed by the faithful Francis. At least the Rudd brothers did not have Knocky's deceitful heart.

He banged on the front door. The sound echoed along the somnolent street, where only drunken revelers staggered along in small groups. It took him three hard series of raps with the knocker before a sleepy maid opened the door a crack.

"I want to see Mrs. Spinks—right this instant." Before the maid could reject him, he'd shouldered his way into the stale den of iniquity. He knew that nothing less than force would get him an appointment with the queen bee of this offensive establishment.

"Ye can't barge in like this, sir!"

"I'm already here. Where is she?"

The maid scuttled ahead of him down a murky corridor and up a set of narrow stairs. On the landing, she knocked timidly on the door. Muffled curses could be heard from inside, and Wyndham took a deep breath and flung the door open. It crashed against the wall. He strode inside, temporarily staggered by the rank air in the chamber. Mrs. Spinks was sitting by the desk, clad only in a transparent nightgown and smoking a cheroot. Her dyed red hair hung in giant curls from under a grimy cap. She lifted her shrewd eyes to the intruder, not in the slightest perturbed by the forceful entry.

"Ah! 'Tis you then. I've waited these two weeks for ye to show up. I ain't got the sparklers."

"I know that," Wyndham said icily and leaned his hands on the desk. Looming over her vulgar face, whitened by cheap powder, he said. "You shall call off your hunt for Knocky Martin. I want his hide. You have no right to it, especially since Temple paid his debt to you. The diamonds are mine, and I fully expect to retrieve them, with or without your help. The fact is, you shall never hold them in your hand again."

Mrs. Spinks's eyelids fluttered under the icy onslaught. "Cor, ye don't mince yer words, guv."

"I mean everything I say. If you lay a hand on Knocky and the diamonds, you'll have to deal with Big Charlie. He made me a promise." Having delivered his speech, Wyndham strode out of the room and ran down the steps. Francis was waiting outside the door with a concerned expression on his face.

"Come, we're going home."

"Reckin ye didn't get what ye came for," Francis said.

"Reckon I didn't."

chapter 17

To clear his head, Wyndham walked all the way from Covent Garden to Berkley Square. The sun had risen over the rooftops, painting the sky a blushing rose. Streaks of gold slanted across the street, and Wyndham thought he ought to make a habit of getting up earlier in the morning to savor the lovely, innocent beginning of the new day.

Before long, he would travel with his young countess into the country. The bucolic idyll of High Wyndham beckoned.

Bone-tired, he went through the back alleys and emerged at the mews. He could always enter through the back entrance, something he never did. But perhaps one of the staff downstairs had news from Knocky.

He climbed down the basement steps and noticed the bundle of rags curled up at the bottom. A beggar, most likely. He was about to rouse the fellow when he noticed the pale gleam of Wyndham livery under the grime. Further scrutiny revealed blond locks and a pert face.

"You—you young varmint!" he shouted and hauled Knocky up by the scruff of his neck.

Knocky kicked out and battered his fists against Wyndham's hard middle until he realized who held him in such a humiliating and punishing grip. He dropped his hands and tried a lopsided grin.

"Good morning, guv, yer Lor'ship. Luvely morn', ain't it?"

"Not for you, it isn't," Wyndham snarled and banged on the locked door. He was locked out of his own house. Finally Xerxes peered through the kitchen window. His lower jaw fell, and he threw himself on the key in the lock.

"I'm ever so sorry—" he began. "Thought it wus the milkmaid. I din't know."

Wyndham marched inside dragging Knocky across the kitchen and up the stairs to the library. Dogwood, still dressed in nightcap, peeked out of the butler's pantry and stared goggle-eyed at the strange goings-on.

Wyndham slammed the library door and shook the young boy. "You deserve the gallows! I spent the small hours of the night in unspeakable dens looking for you and the Wyndham Diamonds. Where did you dispose of them?"

"I din't," Knocky said rebelliously. "I wus tempted, but then I 'membered 'Er Ladyship's sad eyes an' decided me freedom wurn't worth the aggravation. I wus very foolish, melord." He pulled a glittering strand of large diamonds from his pocket.

Wyndham snatched them from him and studied the clasp with its inscription WVNDHAM, 1560, in the light from the window. They were the real article.

"Freedom, Knocky? Would you rather trade your cosseted life here for a life in the streets?" Wyndham asked as he studied the culprit in front of him.

"I bain't used ter bein' closed in a 'ouse most o' th' time, and me fingers itch sumthin' arful at times." He glanced to the floor and shuffled his feet. "But it's been grand 'ere, never had it better. Reckon I can git used to the walls and forgit 'bout nimming wot's not mine—fer 'Er Ladyship's sake. Ain't ever met such a saintly lady."

Wyndham looked down at Knocky's by now serious face. "You could go to the gallows for this, and if not that, you could at least get fifty lashes with the cat o' nines and the stock."

Knocky grinned. "I'll take the lashes, please."

"You damned varmint!" Wrath engulfed Wyndham, and he cuffed the urchin over the ear. Knocky fell onto his backside, but not a sound of protest came to his lips.

"I suppose I'd earned that, an' more," he said, rubbing his ear. "But I ain't goin' ter leave 'Er Ladyship. Not for an'thing."

"Her Ladyship was foolish to offer employment to the likes of you, Knocky, but she wanted to save you from a hard life, so I agreed. If you ever do something like this again, I shall personally kick you out of the house."

Knocky whined. "It ain't 'Er Ladyship wot's foolish, it be ye, guv. Ye don't see that she wud kiss the ground ye tread. Too 'igh an' mighty to see anythin' 'cept the tip o' yer own nose."

Aghast, Wyndham stared at the outspoken urchin and suppressed another urge to give him a blow to the ear. The imp's words touched a chord in his heart, and Wyndham knew he had to find Allegra and make peace with her before it was too late, before her feelings soured.

He reached out, and Knocky placed his hand in Wyndham's. The earl pulled the boy to his feet. "Go. Get away from me and consider yourself lucky. I daresay there's breakfast waiting for you in the servants' hall. And don't show yourself until you've had a bath and changed your clothes."

Knocky grinned from ear to ear. "Yer a downy one, guv. I always thought so." He scampered off.

Dogwood met him outside the door, his face wreathed

in questions. He slung his arm around the boy's shoulders. "Has he misbehaved, my lord?"

Wyndham nodded. "Yes. Your worst suspicions finally came true. I suppose you would like me to throw him out."

Dogwood shook his head. "No, my lord. I admit I've been angry with the boy more often than not, but I've gotten used to him." The butler's old face broke into a smile. "Fact is, I've grown fond of him. Knocky's always eager to give a helping hand."

Wyndham shook his head. "Will wonders never cease?" He moved past the old man and the boy. "Take the devil's spawn to the kitchen and feed him."

The earl ran upstairs, two steps at a time. He cautiously entered his wife's bedchamber and closed the door softly behind him. Thank God, there was no sign of Lucy, the nosy maid.

He trod softly up to the bed and stood staring down at his sleeping wife for a long time. Her face held a paleness that spoke of little sleep. Her eyelids had the puffy and red look of too much crying, and her hand curled defensively around a crumpled handkerchief.

Something expanded in him, a warmth that pushed aside any feeling of frustration and guilt.

He loved her; a new man had taken the place of the old miserable one, a new man whose eyes had been opened to the true values of love.

What he'd felt for Justine was a euphoric pinnacle, a dizzying peak of emotion, while now he recognized that enduring love consisted of small touches of caring that slowly built a foundation of compassion and humble affection. A wise child-woman had taught him that, and as he watched her face so crumpled with misery, he thought his chest was going to explode with tenderness. If not explode, he would surely ascend like one of the hot-air balloons that were displayed at the fairs.

Looking askance at the black kitten rolled up beside her, he sat down beside her and gently took one of her hands into his. "Darling Allegra?" he whispered, and she slowly opened her eyes and stared at him in surprise. He lifted her hand to his lips and covered it with small kisses.

She jerked to a sitting position as if touched by a hot poker. "You ... are here! Are you not angry with me?" She gave him the look of a whipped dog, and his guilt closed an iron band around his chest.

"No—not angry with you. With myself only. I've been such a fool. Took me so long to understand the nature of my feelings." With infinite gentleness he cradled her body close to himself. "I love you more than my life, Allegra. Please say that you harbor some tenderness in your heart for me."

"I do," she whispered into his neck. "I love you so very much. And I am so sorry that I didn't trust you with my problems. I was ... afraid. You can be so very intimidating."

The kitten butted its head against Wyndham's thigh and purred. "I daresay Beau does not unduly harbor fear or jealousy toward me," he said wryly. "So why you?"

"Beau has good sense, which I don't," she said with a downcast face.

"And very sharp claws—when he cares to use them."

"I ... I was afraid you wouldn't speak to me ever again. You were so very angry," she said softly and looked into his silver-blue eyes.

"Yes. I was angry, with Giles, and mostly with myself for presenting such a forbidding facade that you dared not approach me. I hope that you will turn to me with your problems in the future. My place is to protect you from unpleasantness and hardships, and I will be proud to do anything for you."

She burrowed closer to him, all her fear gone now that

he'd bared his heart, his humble love for her. Somehow they had reached an understanding.

Her heart reached out to him, welcomed him, and accepted that she now had to share everything with him, the good and the bad. No one was perfect.

"I would like to take you into my arms," he said, his voice hoarse with emotion.

He would teach her what it meant to be a wife, and she would learn, embarrassed maybe, but eager to find out the secrets of married bliss. "I would like us to be close, to consummate—" Her voice squeaked with mortification, and she could not end the sentence.

He glanced at her in wonder, his face splitting in a delightful grin. "Are you sure that is what you want?"

"Yes . . ."

He slowly released his arms around her and got up to undress. Feeling in his pocket, he pulled out the Wyndham Diamonds. They sparked fire in the early morning light. "I asked you to wear these to the ball. It might be too late for that, but you can wear them—now."

"You found them! I'm so grateful. A terrible load off my shoulders." She smiled and held up her loose hair so that he could clasp the chilly gems around her neck. They were a slight burden, but also a confirmation that she was part of him, the person who would bring the family tree forward. He had clasped them around her neck with love, and love shone in Wyndham's eyes as he finally discarded his clothes and pulled the nightgown over her head. Her heart hammered wildly against her ribs. His skin was velvety soft and his warmth engulfed her as he stretched out beside her and held her naked body close.

As he kissed her, she knew that this was not the end of their marriage ceremony, but the beginning of her married life.